"That was a mistake that won't happen again."

Brianne's cheeks were flushed, and she looked embarrassed and vulnerable from their kiss.

"We have to work together." Then, as if he needed more reasons to keep his distance, he continued, "And I'm much older than you are. I'm not looking for an involvement."

"I see," she murmured, studying her hands rather than him.

Finally her gaze met his. When he looked into her eyes, he remembered the kiss and saw she was remembering, too. He'd been an idiot to give in to the moment. He wouldn't be giving in to the moment again.

As he turned away from Brianne, he tried to shut off everything their kiss had stirred up inside of him. But as he left her staring after him, he felt as if a locked door had been opened.

An open door he might never be able to lock again…

Dear Reader,

October is bringing big changes in the Silhouette and Harlequin worlds. To strengthen the terrific lineup of stories we offer, Silhouette Romance will be moving to four fabulous titles each month.

Don't miss the newest story in this six-book series— MARRYING THE BOSS'S DAUGHTER. In this second title, *Her Pregnant Agenda* (#1690) by Linda Goodnight, Emily Winters is up to her old matchmaking tricks. This time she has a bachelor lawyer and his alluring secretary—a single mom-to-be—on her matrimonial short list.

Valerie Parv launches her newest three-book miniseries, THE CARRAMER TRUST, with *The Viscount & the Virgin* (#1691). In it, an arrogant royal learns a thing or two about love from his secret son's sassy aunt. This is the third continuation of Parv's beloved Carramer saga.

An ornery M.D. is in danger of losing his heart to a sweet young nurse, in *The Most Eligible Doctor* (#1692) by reader favorite Karen Rose Smith. And is it possible to love a two-in-one cowboy? Meet the feisty teacher who does, in Doris Rangel's magical *Marlie's Mystery Man* (#1693), our latest SOULMATES title.

I encourage you to sample all four of these heartwarming romantic titles from Silhouette Romance this month.

Enjoy!

Mavis C. Allen
Associate Senior Editor, Silhouette Romance

Please address questions and book requests to:
Silhouette Reader Service
U.S.: 3010 Walden Ave., P.O. Box 1325, Buffalo, NY 14269
Canadian: P.O. Box 609, Fort Erie, Ont. L2A 5X3

The Most Eligible Doctor
KAREN ROSE SMITH

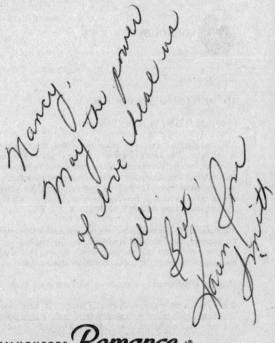

Nancy,
May we power
of love heal us
all.

Best,
Karen Smith

SILHOUETTE *Romance*®

Published by Silhouette Books

America's Publisher of Contemporary Romance

Many thanks to those who helped me
with medical research:
Dr. Steve Goldberg and his wife, Kristi,
as well as paramedics Stephen Bernard and Roger Eib.
Also, thanks to Edie and Mike Hanes,
who helped acquaint me with ice fishing.

 SILHOUETTE BOOKS

ISBN 0-373-19692-X

THE MOST ELIGIBLE DOCTOR

Copyright © 2003 by Karen Rose Smith

Visit Silhouette at www.eHarlequin.com

Printed in U.S.A.

Books by Karen Rose Smith

Silhouette Romance

*Adam's Vow #1075
*Always Daddy #1102
*Shane's Bride #1128
†Cowboy at the Wedding #1171
†Most Eligible Dad #1174
†A Groom and a Promise #1181
The Dad Who Saved
   Christmas #1267
‡Wealth, Power and a
   Proper Wife #1320
‡ Love, Honor and a
   Pregnant Bride #1326
‡Promises, Pumpkins and
   Prince Charming #1332

The Night Before Baby #1348
‡Wishes, Waltzes and a Storybook
   Wedding #1407
Just the Man She Needed #1434
Just the Husband She Chose #1455
Her Honor-Bound Lawman #1480
Be My Bride? #1492
Tall, Dark & True #1506
Her Tycoon Boss #1523
Doctor in Demand #1536
A Husband in Her Eyes #1577
The Marriage Clause #1591
Searching for Her Prince #1612
With One Touch #1638
The Most Eligible Doctor #1692

Silhouette Special Edition

Abigail and Mistletoe #930
The Sheriff's Proposal #1074
His Little Girl's Laughter #1426
Expecting the CEO's Baby #1535

Silhouette Books

The Fortunes of Texas
Marry in Haste...

*Darling Daddies
†The Best Men
‡Do You Take This Stranger?

Previously published under the pseudonym Kari Sutherland

Silhouette Romance

Heartfire, Homefire #973

Silhouette Special Edition

Wish on the Moon #741

KAREN ROSE SMITH,

award-winning author of over forty published novels,
loves to write. She began putting pen to paper in high
school when she discovered poetry as a creative outlet.
Also writing for her high school newspaper, intending to
teach someday, she never suspected crafting emotional
and romantic stories would become her life's work!
Married for thirty-two years, she and her husband reside
in Pennsylvania with their two cats, Ebbie and London.
Readers can e-mail Karen through her Web site at
www.karenrosesmith.com or write to her at P.O. Box
1545, Hanover, PA 17331.

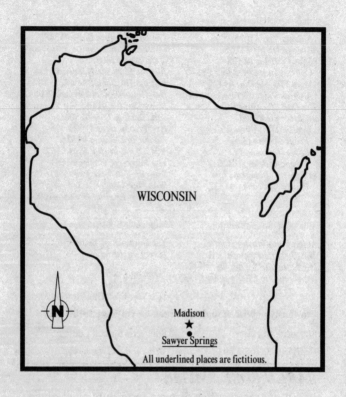

WISCONSIN

Madison
★
<u>Sawyer Springs</u>

All underlined places are fictitious.

Chapter One

Of all days to be late.

Brianne Barrington pulled open the glass door to the Beechwood Family Practice, out of breath, nervous and in a near panic. Brushing her auburn curls from her cold cheek—early January in Wisconsin could be frigid—she wondered if Dr. Jed Sawyer could fire her for tardiness. It was *his* first day…and maybe *her* last. She'd only been working at Beechwood for six months, her first position since graduating from nursing school.

Even in her present state of rushed anxiety, the thought of missing her graduation ceremony and the reason why still brought quick tears. Blinking them away, she hurried into the building.

The waiting room, decorated in soothing tones of blue and green, was already crowded as Brianne raced through one of the two doors leading to examination rooms and offices.

Lily Garrison, her blond hair tied in a low ponytail

today, stepped out of an exam room and asked, "What happened?"

"I set my alarm for p.m. instead of a.m." Most mornings, Lily and her daughter, Megan—Brianne's housemates—were getting ready for their day at the same time she was. But this morning, Lily had a progress-report conference with her five-year-old's teacher.

"Dr. Sawyer's not too happy," Lily warned. "I've been preparing his patients as well as Dr. Olsen's."

After Dr. Olsen had hired Brianne, she'd worked with him, assisting Lily, as well as helping with any phone questions. She'd known that was temporary until the practice hired more doctors.

The thought of Dr. Sawyer's disapproval sent a frisson of panic through her again. "I'm here now. I just have to stow my purse and put on my smock."

The door to examination room 4 suddenly opened and a tall, raven-haired doctor with piercing green eyes stepped out. Brianne could hear a wailing child inside the exam room.

After his penetrating gaze brushed over Lily, it came to rest on Brianne. "Are you my nurse?"

For some mystifying reason, his use of the possessive "my" sent a thrill through her that she didn't understand…and didn't want to feel. Still, she politely extended her hand. "I'm Brianne Barrington. I'm sorry I'm late. Usually I'm a very punctual person, but—"

"Excuses don't carry much weight with me, Miss Barrington. Now that you're here, just do your job. I have a two-year-old in there who won't let me get near her. Is there anything you can do about that?"

His words were a direct challenge to prove herself—right here, right now.

Brianne's breeding demanded that she be ladylike, no matter what. "I can try, Dr. Sawyer." She gazed directly into his very green eyes.

Seconds that seemed like eons ticked by as she felt the space between them fairly crackle with... something tingly that made her terrifically aware of his very broad shoulders, his angular jaw, his imposing male presence. His demeanor showed he wouldn't give an inch. This man didn't back down once he took a stand.

Breaking eye contact, she murmured to Lily, "Could you put this in the office?" and handed her friend her purse. The two nurses shared an office, though each doctor had one of his own.

"No problem," Lily said with a quick glance at Dr. Sawyer.

Then Brianne went into the exam room, checked the chart on the counter for the child's name, and smiled at the little girl, who was sitting on the exam table with her thumb in her mouth. Tears were running down her cheeks.

Brianne greeted their small patient in a soft, friendly voice. "Hi, Cindy."

Warily, the little girl watched her approach.

When Dr. Sawyer stepped into the room once more, Cindy took one look at him and burst into tears again.

"I'm so sorry," the mother exclaimed, putting her arm around her daughter and giving her a tender squeeze. "The last time we were here Dr. Olsen gave her a shot. Your white coat and all reminds her—"

Cindy let out an ear-splitting wail, and Brianne

knew she had to do something fast to help both the baby and the doctor. At the counter, she picked up a pen and drew faces on her thumb and forefinger.

Crossing to the child, she wiggled her fingers and said in a high, lilting voice, "We're the doctor's special helpers. We want to make you smile today."

As she moved her fingers, making them look like puppets, Cindy stopped crying.

Dr. Sawyer slipped out of his lab coat, revealing a white shirt and navy tie with gray dress slacks. But something about him—maybe it was the rugged lines of his face, the over-the-collar length of his hair, and his muscular shoulders—gave Brianne the impression he'd be more comfortable in a flannel shirt and jeans.

As Brianne wiggled her fingers at Cindy, making them talk, the little girl smiled. Then Brianne introduced Dr. Jed. "He's going to check your eyes and ears and throat." At each mention of the body parts, her puppets floated and danced around Cindy's eyes and ears and neck. Then Brianne explained, "Dr. Jed's just going to look for now. I promise."

When Jed Sawyer approached Cindy, she watched him suspiciously, but tears didn't flow this time. Doing her part, Brianne distracted the little girl, and he managed a full examination.

Afterward he said to the mother, "She has an ear infection." Crouching down to Cindy's eye level, he told her in a gentle voice, "Your mommy is going to get you some medicine. It's pink and it tastes sweet. If you take that, your ears will stop hurting and you'll feel a whole lot better."

"Done?" asked the toddler, only concerned about what might come next.

Jed Sawyer smiled wryly. "Yes, we're all done."

Crossing to the cupboard, Brianne took out a canister and offered it to Cindy. Inside were miniature rubber dogs and cats and ducks and birds. "You can pick whichever one you want and take it with you."

Cindy looked over at her mother. The woman nodded encouragingly, "Go ahead, honey."

Dr. Sawyer's little patient chose a yellow cat and held it up to her mom with a grin.

With a last look at Cindy, Jed picked up his lab coat and tossed it over his arm. "Hopefully, the antibiotic will do the trick. But if she isn't better in three days, call us." He patted Cindy on the head. "I'll try to make these visits as painless as possible."

Before he turned away from the child, Brianne saw a flash of something in his eyes—something sad and tearing and deep. Then it vanished. He exited the room, leaving her questioning whether she'd seen anything at all.

After the mother and child left, Brianne picked up charts for the next three patients and went to the waiting room to fetch the first one.

Throughout the morning, she thought she and Dr. Sawyer worked with amazing efficiency, considering they'd never worked together before. Nevertheless, far too often she caught herself staring at him. Her whole body set off warning bells whenever she got near him, and her reaction to Jed Sawyer bothered her. She wasn't in the market for a high-voltage involvement. Being kept in the dark until she was fourteen about the fact that she was adopted, as well as having the people she loved leave her, had left her cautious in more ways than one.

It was midafternoon when the receptionist, Janie Dutton, passed Brianne in the hall. Stopping, she asked, "Are you being asked as many questions about Dr. Sawyer as I am? One woman wanted to know if he was married or eligible before she made her appointment!"

Brianne didn't know whether to be annoyed or to laugh. "I'm getting questions, but since I don't know anything about him, I don't have answers."

"What kind of answers do you need?" Jed asked as he stepped out of his office.

Brianne glanced at Janie, who was obviously as embarrassed as she was.

"I hear the phone ringing," Janie remarked, and hurried off.

"Brianne?" the new doctor asked in a deep voice that told her he wanted an honest answer.

"Dr. Sawyer, I…"

"It's Jed."

"Jed," she murmured. "We're getting questions about you from patients."

"Like…?" he prodded.

Taking a deep breath, she plunged in. "Whether you're married, where you held your last position, how old you are…."

"That's it?" he asked, amusement evident in his tone.

"For starters."

At that he laughed, and the deep richness of it seemed to ripple through Brianne. Shaking his head, he responded, "Since I'm from Sawyer Springs, I know the grapevine is several miles long. So here are the basics. I'm almost forty and worked in Deep River, Alaska, for the past three years." More seriously, he added, "And I'm divorced. If anyone needs to know more than that, tell them to ask me directly.

Now I think we have a patient waiting in exam room 3.'' He nodded toward the door.

Flustered by her reaction to him, Brianne headed for the room at the same time he did. Their shoulders bumped, and his arm went around her to steady her.

Her breath whooshed from her chest. His arm was strong, his woodsy cologne intoxicating. When she gazed up at him, time once again seemed to stand still. There were sparks in his eyes that caused a crazy, wild sensation in her tummy.

As he released her, she tried to regain her composure, warning herself to deny the attraction she felt. *He's too experienced, too masculine, too confident...too everything,* her common sense told her.

Neither of them said a word as Jed stepped into the exam room and she followed.

At the end of the day, Jed told Dr. Olsen he would take the last patient, who was a walk-in, if Brianne didn't mind staying. She didn't mind. Besides, she wanted to show her new boss that her tardiness this morning wasn't a sign of lack of dedication to her profession.

Around six-thirty, they'd finally finished with the patient, who'd cut his arm and needed stitches. Switching off the computer printer, Brianne watched the man's wife lead him outside.

When Jed stepped into the front office, he was wearing his suit coat and looked distinguished and handsome. Brianne felt her stomach skitter again, and decided she was simply hungry.

She lifted her coat from a hook on the wall. ''This has been a long first day for you.''

''I was sometimes on duty forty-eight hours at a time in Deep River.''

"You were short on staff?"

With a wry smile, he took her coat from her. "Staff consisted of me and a nurse. There were only ninety-nine residents in the village."

As he held her coat for her, she slid her arms into the sleeves, then turned around. "Did you enjoy your work there?" she asked. They were mere inches apart. She could see the small lines around his eyes and mouth, the few strands of silver at his temples.

His gaze found hers and stayed for a few moments. "Practicing there was challenging." He cleared his throat. "All the supplies had to be flown in."

Realizing he'd evaded her question, she had the feeling he didn't want to talk about anything personal. Even though he'd given her the basics earlier, he didn't seem to want to divulge more than that. "I can see how practicing in a remote village would be challenging."

The atmosphere in the office was thick with tension as they stood there. Brianne stepped away from him so she could think straight. She wanted to apologize once more for this morning. "I'm sorry about my lateness today. I don't have a good excuse. I have a digital alarm and I mistakenly set it for p.m. instead of a.m. On top of that, I didn't sleep well and I was late awakening. Lily and Megan usually make enough noise to—"

"Why didn't you sleep well?" he interrupted.

Though he apparently didn't like answering personal questions, he didn't mind asking them. She might as well tell him the truth. "I was anxious about today. Working with a new doctor and all."

"From your performance, I don't see why you

were anxious. You're good with the patients and more than competent in the exam room.''

The compliment blindsided her and she felt her cheeks grow warm. ''Thank you.''

''You're welcome. I'm sorry I was gruff this morning. I didn't sleep well, either, last night. My father has insomnia and rattles around in the kitchen at 2:00 a.m.''

''He should try chamomile tea,'' she suggested impulsively.

Warm humor lit up Jed's eyes. ''He's set in his ways and doesn't take advice well. But I'll mention the tea.'' As she crossed to the doorway, he offered, ''If you're on the way out, I'll walk you to your car.''

''Oh, that's not necessary.''

''I feel responsible keeping you this late. I want to make sure you're safely on your way home before I leave.''

In spite of safety alarms in her heart warning her to keep her distance from Jed Sawyer, she was disappointed there was nothing personal about his offer. She realized he was simply one of those men who was a protector.

She gathered up her purse. ''I have to set the security system.''

Nodding, he let her precede him out of the office.

A few minutes later, when they stepped outside into the black, early January night, Brianne took in a huge breath of the cold air. ''I guess Wisconsin weather is mild compared to Alaska's.''

Jed walked beside her, his words coming out with white puffs of vapor. ''Deep River was a whole different world. We had wind chill of fifty-eight below in December. Yet when the northern lights lit up the sky, none of the rest seemed to matter.''

She thought about Alaska and the aurora borealis...and Jed watching it. Then she motioned toward her car, the only one in the parking lot. ''You walked?'' she asked.

''I'm about six blocks away.'' He was staring at her car. The parking lot lights flowed over the white foreign sports car as if spotlighting it.

''Would you like a ride?'' she asked. ''I can drop you off.''

''Thanks, but I enjoy walking.''

From what she could tell, Jed was extremely fit, and she wondered if he did more than walk. He was still eyeing her car.

She opened the driver's door, and the smell of leather was noticeable.

He glanced inside, then focused once more on her.

They were standing very close. So close that Brianne found it hard to breathe again. He was a good seven inches taller than she was, and she felt fragile, small and out of her depth standing before him. She tipped her chin up a little, and she could have sworn he leaned a bit closer.

Neither of them spoke as the pines along the building swayed in a breeze and a truck rattled down the street. Her heart beat faster than it ever had.

Then Jed lifted his head and put a few inches between them. With his hand on the frame of the sports car, he said, ''This is a beautiful car. You don't find many of them in Wisconsin.''

She felt memories flood over her, and heat came to her cheeks despite the cold. ''It was a graduation gift from my parents,'' she said in a low voice.

"You must have very generous parents."

Her parents. Irrevocably gone. Unbearably missed. Two days before her graduation, as they drove to her college, a tractor trailer had swerved into them.

Her voice caught as she managed to answer, "They *were* very generous. They're gone now."

Seeing the uncertainty on Jed's face at her words, she decided to leave to take care of the awkwardness she'd created.

"I'll see you tomorrow. Have a good night." Sliding quickly into the bucket seat, she closed the door and switched on the ignition.

Dr. Jed Sawyer stepped away from her car.

Quickly, she backed up, veered to the right and out of the parking lot, trying to keep heartache at bay.

On Saturday morning, after Brianne had run a few errands, she returned to the Victorian house that had become her home. After her parents died, seven months ago, she'd been lost in their huge house. She'd taken the job at Beechwood Family Practice a month after graduation and had met Lily Garrison, a divorced mother who'd been looking for a housemate so she and Megan could more easily meet their bills each month. Lily and Megan had provided Brianne with a safe harbor, and they now felt like family.

The house's wraparound porch with its yellow railing brought a smile to Brianne's face, as it always did. After parking along the street—there was only a one-car detached garage in the back—Brianne picked up her dry cleaning from the seat beside her and ran up the three wooden steps.

As she stepped inside the living room with its shiny hardwood floor, colorful rag rugs and big-cushioned, overstuffed turquoise-and-red furniture, the smell of cinnamon wafted around her. Carefully hooking her dry cleaning over a closet door hinge, she headed for the kitchen and was surprised by the activity there.

"We're having a party," five-year-old Megan called as she pressed a cookie cutter into bread slices.

"A party?" Brianne asked. She had been up and out before Lily and Megan had awakened this morning. Lily hadn't said anything about a party last evening.

Lily's blond waves, loose around her face now, swished against her cheek as she looked up from her cutting board, where she was slicing celery. "Last night when Doug and I were talking, I mentioned Jed Sawyer."

Doug was a computer technician Lily had been dating for months now. Despite her good intentions to leave thoughts of Jed Sawyer at Beechwood, Brianne *was* interested in anything Doug had had to say about the rugged doctor. Ever since that night almost a week ago when Jed had made the comment about her car, they'd worked efficiently together, but politely, with no personal conversations. He didn't seem to engage in truly personal conversation with anyone.

"What did Doug say?" Brianne asked.

"The gist of it was that it must be difficult for Jed to come back home and live with his dad after all these years. So...I thought it would be nice to have an open house for him. Just a welcome home get-together. I remembered you said you didn't have plans for tomorrow, so I invited Dr. Olsen and his wife, Sue and Janie and their husbands."

Sue in billing helped Janie manage the practice's office. It was just like Lily to want to help Jed feel comfortable being in Sawyer Springs again, and to impulsively throw a party.

"You didn't make plans, did you?" Lily asked. "I told everyone to come around three."

"I'm free." Brianne's heart fluttered as she thought about Jed, here, in a casual atmosphere. "Did you invite Dr. Sawyer?" she asked with a smile.

Lily made a face at her. "Yep. Called him this morning. He said he'll stop in, though he can't stay long. I think he's just leaving himself an out in case he doesn't want to stay."

"What makes you say that?" Brianne asked, wandering over to snitch a carrot from the growing stack of vegetables.

"He's a loner," Lily said solemnly. "I can tell. Did you know he practiced as a plastic surgeon in Los Angeles before he took that position in Alaska?"

"How do you *know* that?"

Lily gave her a mysterious smile. "I have my ways."

Brianne laughed.

Glancing at her housemate over her shoulder, Lily confided, "I'm not really Sherlock Holmes. I got a glimpse of Jed Sawyer's résumé. Dr. Olsen happened to have it in his hand yesterday when he was talking to me."

"Jed said he was divorced. I wonder how long he was married?" Brianne mused.

Lily tilted her head and cocked a brow. "You're working for the man, maybe you could ask him."

"He doesn't talk about himself much." Brianne suddenly knew she was sounding too interested.

"Do you wish he would?" Lily asked more gently.

"No. It's better this way…that we keep a strictly

professional relationship. After all, he's my boss.''
Besides that Jed Sawyer was obviously experienced.
She was inexperienced. That was her choice. She'd
had a lot of losses in her life and because of them
she tried to protect her heart.

She'd felt totally adrift when, at fourteen, she'd
found a private investigator's report in the attic. It had
stated that her biological mother had taken her to a
church pew in Madison and died a few months later
from pneumonia because she'd been homeless and
living on the streets.

Since Brianne's parents hadn't told her about any
of it, she'd felt betrayed. Since her birth mother had
left her in the church, she'd felt abandoned. Brianne
had depended heavily on her childhood friend, Bobby
Spivak, during that confusing time. He'd been her
best friend since kindergarten. But in their senior
year, they were discussing getting engaged and going
to the same college when Bobby had been diagnosed
with leukemia. She'd lost him eighteen months later.

And seven months ago, she'd lost her parents, too.
Over and over again she'd learned that love hurt in
so many ways. Yet…she also knew it was life-giving.
Bobby's doctors had said he had six months to live.
He'd lived a year past that, and Brianne's heart told
her that love had kept him with them.

Still, she was afraid of loving…and losing once
more. Giving her heart away wasn't in her plans anytime soon, if ever.

When Brianne thought of Jed Sawyer, she realized
her relationship with Bobby had been the epitome of
safety. Their love had been born of friendship and
hadn't yet developed into burning passion. Jed, on the
other hand, was so intense that all she thought about

amid the tingles she felt around him was passion. That spelled trouble with a capital *T*. She wouldn't let a few unruly hormones run away with her good sense.

Ending the conversation and putting a lid on her thoughts, she asked Lily, "So what can I do to help get ready for tomorrow?"

If she stayed busy, tomorrow and seeing Jed again in a relaxed setting wouldn't make her so jittery.

Mingling.

Jed had once known how to do it like a pro. Back in L.A., he and his partners had been invited to cocktail parties with movie stars, investment bankers, models. He'd been able to talk to anyone about anything. But then his life had fallen apart and talking had become too much of an effort. The position in Alaska had been a godsend, but because of it, he'd grown rusty at socializing.

Lily Garrison crossed to him, a tray balanced on her hand. "Try the crab quiches. I found the recipe on the Internet."

Jed took one, bit into it and grinned. "Maybe you should go into catering as a sideline."

"I think I have my hands full with work and Megan. But I'll keep that in mind."

Suddenly Jed's attention was drawn to Brianne as she entered the living room. She stood by the built-in bookshelves for a moment, looking uncertain. Her auburn, shoulder-length curls bobbed around her face with the slightest movement of her head. Her aquamarine eyes were the wonderful color of the sea. Ever since that night by the car, he'd wanted to talk to her again about more than work, but the clinical atmosphere at Beechwood hadn't seemed right to delve into the subject of her parents. And the stirrings of desire he'd felt whenever they were around each other had deterred him from seeking her out privately.

When Brianne's gaze passed over the room as if she was deciding which conversation to enter, her eyes met his. She quickly looked away, turned around and retreated to the kitchen.

Finishing the miniature quiche in a quick bite, Jed said to Lily, "Excuse me, will you? There's someone I need to talk to."

Lily's eyes twinkled. "I'll catch you later." Then she moved along to another group with her tray.

Jed strode through the dining room into the kitchen, where he found Brianne scooping coffee into a filter.

"You and Lily went to a lot of trouble today."

Startled, she looked up, and her cheeks became a little rosier. "It wasn't that much trouble. Are you enjoying yourself?"

"The truth is, I'm having to readjust to a party mode. I haven't been to one for a few years."

"Since you took the job in Alaska?"

"Yes."

There was an awkward silence, and Jed knew he had to be the one to fill it. "I didn't mean to upset you on Monday night. I shouldn't have pried into your life. Living alone in a cabin wore off my civilized veneer. I'm sorry about your parents." After she'd mentioned losing her parents, Jed had remembered his dad filling him in on some of the things that had happened in Sawyer Springs the past couple of years. Skyler Barrington had been a lawyer, her husband Edward a cardiologist. They had both come from money and their name was well known in the town. Brianne had inherited all of their wealth and could be considered an heiress. Jed was a bit puzzled why she was working as a nurse at Beechwood when she could be traveling the world, living anywhere she pleased.

Her gaze was vulnerable as she looked up at him. "Thank you. It's been less than a year since their accident, and I—"

Brianne never got to finish because Megan came running in and threw her arms around Brianne's waist. Her hair was lighter blond than her mother's, and Lily had attached a barrette over each of her daughter's temples. In the crook of her arm, Megan carried a rag doll dressed in blue-and-pink gingham, with red yarn hair.

Looking at the beautiful child made Jed's heart clench. He wondered if he'd ever be able to be comfortable around children again. Trisha had been almost three when she'd drowned, and being around kids always made his memories more of a burden.

Megan stood on her tiptoes and crooked her finger at Brianne, glancing shyly at Jed. "Can I have another cookie?" she almost whispered. "Mommy said I could. There aren't any more on the tray. So she said I should ask you."

When Brianne smiled, her face lit up, as did her eyes and everything about her. Jed could tell this child meant a lot to her.

"We'll have to do something about an empty cookie tray," Brianne agreed. "Sure, you can have another one."

"Can I take the lid off the cookie jar?" Megan asked eagerly.

"Maybe Dr. Sawyer can lift you up. I'll hold Penelope for you."

Brianne looked at Jed as if she was making an everyday request. He realized she was, and he shouldn't make a big deal of it. He tried to keep his expression blank. "Where's the cookie jar?" he asked gruffly.

Pulling a gingerbread boy jar from behind the coffeepot, Brianne nudged it near the edge of the counter with her elbow as she tucked the rag doll under her arm and filled the coffee carafe with water.

Megan ran over to Jed and held her arms up to him. His chest was so tight he could hardly breathe. Clasping her around the waist, he lifted her until she could reach the jar, telling himself not to feel...not to think...not to remember.

But Brianne had turned off the water now and was looking at him curiously. He realized something showed—something he didn't want her to see.

After Megan lifted off the gingerbread boy's head, Brianne took out about a dozen cookies to replenish the empty tray. The little girl replaced the lid very carefully, and Brianne handed her a cookie. Megan glanced over her shoulder at Jed. "You can put me down now."

He gently settled her on the floor again.

When she looked up at him, her smile was as sparkling as her blue eyes. "Thank you. Do you want one?"

"No. Not now."

She nodded as if she understood. "You have to eat your vegetables before you can eat cookies." After Brianne handed Megan her doll, the little girl ran out of the kitchen, leaving them alone again.

"Dr. Sawyer, are you all right?"

"It's Jed," he brusquely reminded her.

With her concerned expression, her beautifully

curved lips, her pretty heart-shaped face, he knew staying away from Brianne was his best course of action. Besides the fact that he was much too old for her—Dr. Olsen had mentioned she was twenty-three—he knew her background was probably a carbon copy of his ex-wife's. After all, Brianne was a Barrington. Getting to know her outside of their working relationship was *not* a good idea.

"I'm fine," he assured her now. "But I have to be going."

"So soon? Have you even had any cake?" She pointed to the table holding a frosted cake with Welcome written on it.

"No, I haven't. But everyone here can enjoy it. I really do appreciate you and Lily welcoming me back to Sawyer Springs. If I don't see Lily on my way out, please tell her how grateful I am." He knew his voice was flat. He knew he didn't have a decent excuse to give for leaving. Yet none of that mattered. He wasn't ready to be around mothers and children...or a woman who seemed to be thawing his frozen libido.

As he left the kitchen, Brianne called, "I'll see you in the morning." He lifted his hand in acknowledgment that he'd heard her. Then he headed for the door, deciding he should have stayed in Alaska.

Chapter Two

As Brianne filed patient charts late Monday afternoon, she quickly glanced out the window. Snow had been falling heavily since midmorning. Everyone else had left, and she was waiting for Jed to finish with his last chart. He'd been distant today, and she wondered again what had gone through his mind yesterday afternoon at the party—and why he'd left so abruptly. The only personal conversation they'd had was "good morning." Everything else had had to do with work.

Still…Brianne found the man intriguing, in spite of herself. Working around him minute by minute, hour by hour, she found thoughts taking shape in her head she'd never had before. Thoughts of a man and woman kissing, touching…

With a blast of mid-January wind, the door in the reception area burst open and a burly figure stomped in. Brianne was used to walk-ins by now, but she was also a bit worried about how long another appointment would take, and driving home in the deepening snow.

The elderly man tracked slush from his black galoshes through the waiting room as he came to the receptionist's window. He wore an orange hunter's cap, and he pushed it high on his brow now as he gazed at her from beneath bushy gray brows. His face was lined, his square jaw beard-stubbled. The loose, red-plaid wool jacket he was wearing made him look bigger and burlier than he actually was, she noted.

Closing the sliding metal door of the files, Brianne crossed to the glass window and opened it. "Can I help you?"

His green eyes passed over her appraisingly. "Just point me in the direction of Jed Sawyer."

She would never let an unverified patient into the exam area. "Do you have an appointment with Dr. Sawyer?"

"I don't need an appointment. I'm his father."

Brianne smiled at once. She could see the resemblance now in the high cheekbones and the broad brow. "Dr. Sawyer is finishing patient notes. I'll get him."

But before Brianne could step back from the window, Jed entered the office and spotted his father. "Dad. What are you doing out in this?"

His father shrugged. "I needed rock salt for the sidewalk if this ices up. Since you walked here, I thought you might appreciate a ride. You'd better buy yourself a four-wheel-drive truck like I've got if you intend to stay here."

Jed frowned at his father's words. "I'm used to walking in the snow. I have a few more—"

The shrill tone of the phone ringing broke the tension between the two men. Relieved, Brianne answered it. "Beechwood Family Practice."

"It's Lily," her friend said quickly. "Are you leaving soon?"

"I'd better if I don't want to spend the night."

"That's why I'm calling. A report came over the radio that the power is out on our side of town. So Megan and I are going to stay with Mom tonight."

Bea Brinkman, Lily's mother, was also her child care provider. She watched Megan whenever Lily had to work.

"Will the power be out all night?" Brianne asked.

"They don't know. Do you want to come here and stay with us? Mom says you're more than welcome."

"I don't know if my car can make it to the farm. Are the roads plowed?"

"Not yet. I could try to come get you."

"No! I don't want you to take that chance. I can stay here."

Jed's father gruffly but adamantly broke into their conversation. "Young lady, that's a bad idea. A young woman like you alone in a deserted building at night? Why don't you come have supper with us, and then we'll take you wherever you have to go. My truck can get through anything."

"Who was that?" Lily asked, apparently hearing bits and pieces of the conversation.

"It's Dr. Sawyer's father. He, uh, suggested I have dinner with them and then he'll bring me to the farm." Brianne looked over at Jed.

He wasn't exactly frowning, but he didn't look happy about the turn of events, either. Not hesitating, though, he agreed with his father. "You can't stay here alone. Come over to the house with us. We've got plenty of room. If the roads are too difficult, you can stay the night.''

"I don't want to put you to any trouble.''

"It won't be any trouble,'' he said gruffly. "Dad's right. If the power is out, we probably *should* be going before this gets any worse.''

Brianne certainly didn't want Lily driving in this snowstorm, or for that matter, Jed's dad taking a chance driving out to the farm. She knew she'd be perfectly safe with the two men. It was an instinctive knowing.

After only a few more seconds of hesitation, she said to Lily, "I'll be at Dr. Sawyer's if you need me. If the snow stops and the roads are plowed, I'll join you later.''

"Are you sure that's what you want to do?'' Lily asked, concern in her voice.

Looking at Jed again, Brianne felt the stirring of excitement that always happened whenever she was around him. Reminding herself that going to the Sawyers' house was a practical solution, she assured her friend, "Yes, that's what I want to do. Tell your mom thanks for the offer. I'll get back to you later.''

When she hung up the phone, she said brightly, "I guess that's settled, then. But you have to let me help you with dinner.''

"We won't turn down that offer.'' Jed's dad gave her a sly smile and extended his hand to her. "Al Sawyer. And you're…''

"Brianne Barrington.''

"Edward Barrington's daughter?'' Al asked with a lift of his bushy brows.

"Yes. Did you know him?''

Nodding, he explained, "I went to see him

once…for my heart. Some kind of rhythm problem. He gave me medicine that fixed it right up. I liked him. He wasn't one of those docs who spend two minutes with you and they're on their way."

"Dad was a good listener."

"I couldn't believe it when I heard about the accident. It's a shame you're an only child. Brothers or sisters help at a time like that."

Shifting from one booted foot to the other, Al suddenly looked uncomfortable, as if he didn't know what to say next.

Jed stepped in. "Dad, why don't you get the truck heated up? We'll be right out."

The older man seemed grateful that his son had cut off the conversation. "Sure thing. I'll probably have to clean off the windshield again, so take your time."

After Al went through the door, Brianne asked Jed, "Are you sure you want me to come?"

"You grew up in Sawyer Springs, didn't you?" he asked, instead of answering.

"Yes, I did."

"Then you know that neighbor helps neighbor here."

"Yes, I know that, but…"

"It's one of the reasons I came back here, Brianne. Dad was the main reason. But I lived in L.A. before I went to Alaska, and it's much different out there. Families are mobile units. Neighbors come and go. It's not at all like here."

"You came back because you like Sawyer Springs?"

"I came back because it was time." His gaze passed over her again, and it was as if he was studying every light freckle on her nose. "I don't want you out in this storm any more than Dad does. And this building is no place for you to be on a night like this. I'll warn you, though—Dad's a little rough around the edges and pretty blunt sometimes.''

"Unlike you?" she asked with a smile.

He shook his head and chuckled. "You got me there. I guess what you're saying is, if you can put up with *me,* you can put up with *him.*"

"I enjoy working with you, Jed," she said sincerely. "It's not a hardship."

Tilting his head, he asked, "Are you always this honest?"

"I try to be. Tactful, too, I hope," she added teasingly.

"I see." With amusement in his eyes, he took a step closer. "There's honest and blunt, and honest and *tactful.* I'll try to remember that."

They were standing less than a foot apart. She could almost feel his intensity, sense his heat, see his defenses. For a moment she'd made him laugh.

Now he became serious again, his voice low. "Get your coat. I'll make sure everything's locked up."

Five minutes later he held the truck door for her as she climbed in beside his father. The truck seat was roomy, but once Jed shut his door, his down jacket touched the sleeve of her camel wool coat. His trousered leg brushed against hers and Brianne's breath caught. What was it about this man that excited her so? Although she might be intrigued by him, this excursion to his house could be a colossal mistake. Being impulsive wasn't in her nature. Yet around him, she almost felt reckless. That was dangerous territory for a virgin who didn't want to lose her heart.

"Here we go," Al said, windshield wipers clearing the snow away while heat poured from the vents.

When he pulled onto the street through the six-inch-deep snow, Brianne rocked against Jed. He didn't move and neither did she, and the heat between them seemed a lot more intense than what was coming out of the vents.

Was it purely her imagination? Certainly, he wasn't affected by her the way she was affected by him. Yet when she glanced at his profile, she saw the nerve in his jaw twitch.

There was no one on the roads, and a short time later, Al pulled up in front of a one-and-a-half story house. It was painted blue and accented by black shutters. The porch light was glowing, so apparently the power lines in this part of town hadn't been damaged.

Jed opened his door and climbed out, waiting for Brianne. The snow was getting deeper, and when she jumped from the truck, she discovered it was over the top of her leather boots. She wrinkled her nose at the cold sensation, realizing that by the time she walked to the house, her feet would be wet.

Jed sized up the situation promptly and swung her into his arms.

"What are you doing?" she gasped. He'd moved so quickly, she felt as if she were floating in midair. She wrapped her arms around his neck for security's sake.

"You need a pair of *real* boots."

"These *are* real boots. I've worn them all winter."

"Real boots don't make a fashion statement. They're snug around the calves and go to your knees."

He had a point. Although it snowed quite a bit, she

wasn't out in it very much. She liked to look feminine and stylish. She did own a pair of tie boots with lamb's wool inside, but they would have looked hideous with her skirt.

Thoughts of boots vanished as Jed carried her to the front stoop. He was as solid as a granite cliff. Held against him as she was, she could feel the breadth of his shoulders and the strength of his arms. Under the overhang of the porch, there was only about an inch of snow. He set her down lightly, as if she were fragile enough to break. She felt so small beside him. So slight. So feminine. The green depths of his eyes mesmerized her as they stood close together.

He fingered a stray curl along her cheek, and she thought she'd melt right there on his porch. "Hats are a good idea in this kind of weather, too," he advised huskily.

"I'll remember that the next time it snows," she murmured, knowing that coming here with Jed was a very big mistake.

Al suddenly came up behind them. "Want my key?"

Quickly Jed dug into his jacket pocket. "Nope. I've got mine." He opened the door and let Brianne enter before him.

As she took a quick look around, Jed shrugged out of his coat and switched on a light. "It's like stepping back into the fifties, isn't it?"

Glancing around the interior of the house, she saw what he meant. There was warm wood flooring, but it didn't have the finish modern floors had. The brick fireplace was simple, without a hearth, but with an alcove to store wood next to it. A gold-and-green flowered sofa sat against one wall, near a comfortable-looking tweed recliner that had seen years' worth of use. Beyond the living room she could see the kitchen, with its linoleum floor, and yellow and white ceramic tiles behind the appliances and sink. The counters were gold swirl and the cabinets birch.

"There wasn't anything wrong with the fifties," Al mumbled.

After Brianne removed her coat, Jed took it and hung it in the closet beside his. "I'll get a fire started. The house has always been drafty."

Brianne heard Al harumph as he went into the kitchen and hung his jacket on a rack there.

When she crossed to the fireplace, she studied the pictures on the TV console next to it. "You have a brother and a sister?" she asked, looking at a family portrait, the only one in the room from what she could see.

As Jed touched a long match to the kindling, he answered, "Yes."

"Older or younger?" She knew she was pushing, but she wanted to know more about this man.

"They're both older."

"Do they live around here?"

Crouching down, Jed placed two logs on the fire. "No. None of us could wait to escape small-town life in Sawyer Springs. Ellie is out in California producing documentaries, and Chris is a colonel in the army now."

"You're all successful. I'll bet that makes your parents proud."

With a last look at the dancing flames, Jed closed the mesh screen, stood and faced her. "Mom instilled the idea in us that we could rise above anything, be whatever we wanted to be. She died during my residency, but she knew we were all on our way.''

So Jed knew how it felt to lose a parent. Thinking about it, Brianne felt she'd lost hers twice—once when she'd found out she was adopted, because nothing had been the same after that, and then again after the accident. ''I'll bet your dad's proud of what you've accomplished.''

Jed turned away and gazed into the fire for a few moments. ''I'm not sure what Dad feels. And my idea of success has changed over the past few years.'' A haunted shadow crossed his face again.

Wanting to be honest with him, she admitted, ''I know you were a plastic surgeon in L.A. before you went to Alaska. Did something happen to—''

Al returned to the living room then, unaware that he was interrupting. With a broad smile, he addressed Brianne. ''We've got leftover rotisserie chicken from the deli and a bag of potatoes. Anything you can cook up with that?'' Al Sawyer apparently was the kind of man who assumed that all women knew how to cook.

''Dad, you can't expect Brianne—''

''That sounds like the beginnings of a scalloped-potato-and-chicken casserole to me. What do you think about that?'' she asked seriously.

Grinning, Al nodded. ''Now you're talkin'. I knew it was a good idea bringin' you along home.''

Brianne laughed and Jed just shook his head. ''You really know how to win a girl over, Dad.''

''Maybe you should try it sometime,'' his father replied.

Jed's face went still and the hint of a smile vanished. But his tone was even when he said, ''Dad keeps a stash of frozen cakes in the downstairs freezer. I'll get one of those for dessert before we all start peeling potatoes.''

Deciding to put her best foot forward—what trouble could she get into cooking supper?—Brianne smiled at Jed's father. ''Mr. Sawyer, why don't you show me around your kitchen?''

As he jammed his hands into the pockets of his coveralls, he muttered, ''It's Al. Come on, and I'll show you where everything is.''

After supper, washing dishes while Brianne dried, Jed tried to figure out why he felt turned inside out whenever he was around her. Her presence stirred up emotions he hadn't felt in years. He told himself she was young and beautiful, and that's all it was.

He was placing the last dish in the drainer when his father went to the back door and looked out. ''The snow shows no sign of stopping anytime soon. I think I'll go out and shovel the front walk.''

''I bought the snowblower so you don't have to do that, Dad. I'll take it out later for its first pass.''

''That thing runs away with me,'' Al grumbled. ''I prefer a shovel.''

''You should prefer the living room in front of the fire, and let me take care of it.''

His face reddening, Al demanded, ''And just what happens if I let you take care of everything and then you leave and I'm stuck with it again? I'll be out of shape and not used to countin' on myself. If you're so dad-blasted set on running the snowblower, I'll go upstairs and work on that jigsaw puzzle in my room.''

''Mr. Sawyer?'' Brianne said as he started toward the living room.

Al gave her a look that said she was supposed to call him by his first name.

"Al," she amended. "I don't want to disrupt your evening. If you want to watch TV—"

"You're not disrupting anything. I'm almost finished with that puzzle and I want to see it all put together. Jed will find you anything you need for tonight. If I don't see you before, I'll see you in the morning." He left the kitchen abruptly without saying good-night to his son.

Jed took the dish towel from Brianne's hands. "Let the rest drip dry. Would you like a glass of brandy?"

The house *was* drafty, and the idea of a glass of brandy in front of the fire with Jed was appealing. "Sure."

A few minutes later as he joined her on the sofa, he handed her a small snifter, took a sip of his, set it on the coffee table and ran his hand through his hair. She could tell the interchange with his father was still frustrating him.

"Your dad doesn't take to change easily?"

"*That's* an understatement. Every time I try to do something for him, there's a battle."

"It sounds as if he doesn't think you'll be staying here."

Shifting toward her, Jed replied, "I'm not sure I will be. How about you? Where do you want your career to take you?"

Before she'd accepted the position at the Beechwood, she'd applied for a job with Project Voyage— a team of doctors and nurses who volunteered their time helping children in South America. But she hadn't heard from them, and when the position at the family practice had opened, she'd decided it was just what she needed while she settled her parents' estate and got her life in some kind of order. "I'm not sure where I want it to take me."

"Why didn't you go to med school and follow in your father's footsteps?" Jed's gaze was probing.

"I'm not sure how to explain." She thought of Bobby and how she'd helped nurse him every day after school. "I like caring for patients, not just listening to their symptoms and prescribing medication. I saw my father's life—how he wanted to give more time to each patient but couldn't always, the kind of hours he kept, being called out in the middle of the night. If I ever have a family, I'd like to keep working. But I also want to be there for them. Do you know what I mean?"

Jed knew exactly what she meant. Caroline had accused him often of not being available, of his patients always coming first. He didn't feel it was true. Especially after their daughter was born. Trisha had been the light of his life, and sometimes he'd thought Caroline was jealous of that. She'd been a pampered, spoiled rich girl, used to being the center of attention. Unfortunately, he hadn't realized that until after he'd married her.

Brianne came from money, too. Nevertheless, he'd felt her compassion, could see what a caring nature she had. Maybe that's why his desire for her was only part of what was going on. Her soft, bronze-colored sweater had a round neck that molded to her creamy throat. Her calf-length wool skirt draped enticingly over her slender hips and curvy legs. When he'd carried her earlier and her arms had gone around his neck, he'd realized he'd been alone for a long time now.

The flaming wood in the fireplace popped and crackled. The sip of brandy he'd taken made a burning path down his throat. Yet the heat inside him had nothing to do with the fire or the brandy.

Brianne was looking up at him with such complete absorption...

"Brianne," he said huskily.

She didn't move, just kept studying his face, his lips, as if she was as curious as he was about the chemistry brewing between them.

Bending his head, he savored the moment of wanting her...of needing her. He reveled in the feeling as his blood started racing faster and his hunger built. His lips hovered over hers and he heard her sigh, then catch her breath. But she didn't move away.

I feel alive again, he thought as his lips touched hers.

Fascinated by the soft curls and their fiery color, Jed was unable to resist sliding his hand into Brianne's hair. His tongue instinctively slipped between her lips, and when her hands went to his shoulders, he brought her closer. Breathing her in, he delved into her mouth, giving himself up to the kiss, to Brianne, the fire and the brandy.

Numb as he'd been to his physical needs for the past four years, Jed felt more aroused now than he'd ever been in his life. Brianne's soft moan, her surrender to the desire between them, her sweet beauty, spun him into turmoil and excitement and hunger.

It was the hunger that stopped him—the soul-deep, aching hunger that he knew he could never satisfy. He couldn't use Brianne as a Band-aid. He wouldn't take advantage of her. He shouldn't become involved at all.

Tearing away from her, controlling the mind-drugging sensations of holding her, tasting her and kissing her, he shifted until there was space between them.

He waited until he saw the sensual haze in her eyes dissipate a bit. "That was a mistake that won't happen again."

Her cheeks were flushed, and she looked embarrassed and vulnerable.

"We have to work together," he added. Then, as if he needed more reasons to keep his distance, he continued, "And I'm much older than you are. I'm not looking for an involvement."

"I see," she murmured, studying her hands now, rather than him.

He stood. "I'd better see to that snowblower. Your room is the one at the top of the stairs. I put towels on the bed."

Trying to act casual, she repositioned a sofa pillow. "Do you think we'll be able to get out in the morning?"

"I'm hoping the plow will come through."

Finally her gaze met his. When he looked into her eyes, he remembered the kiss and saw she was remembering, too. He'd been an idiot to give in to the moment. He wouldn't do so again.

As he turned away from Brianne, he tried to shut off everything that kiss had stirred up inside him. But as he left her staring into the fire, took his jacket from the closet and went out into the swirling snow, he felt as if a locked door had been opened.

And he might never be able to lock it again.

The mattress was lumpy, but that wasn't the reason Brianne couldn't sleep in the simple pine bed. Her nose and hands and feet were cold. To distract herself, she thought back to the memory of Jed's kiss. Why had she let it happen? Why hadn't she backed away? He'd given her time. But she'd been overcome by curiosity, by a sense of adventure she'd never experienced before.

The howl of the wind sounded through the window, and she shivered.

There was a knock on the door to her room, then it opened. "Brianne?"

She recognized Jed's voice immediately. "I'm awake."

When he came into the room dressed in a white T-shirt with gray sweatpants, he was carrying a flashlight. "Now our power is out, too. The temperature in the house has dropped. Do you want to come down and sleep on the sofa by the fire?"

"What about your dad?"

"He's sound asleep and snoring. I laid a down-filled quilt over him and that should do the trick. But we only have one of those."

"What time is it?" she asked, unable to see her watch.

"It's three. If you get warm, you could still catch a couple of hours of sleep before you have to get up."

"All right." Suddenly she realized the predicament she was in. "Can you turn around while I dress?" She'd crawled under the covers in her slip. Her sweater and skirt lay over the chair.

His gaze went to the clothes and then back to her. "I'd go on down, but you're going to need the flashlight. Just tell me when you're finished." Then he turned and faced the door.

Brushing her tousled curls off her forehead, Brianne realized her hair was an absolute mess. But without her comb, brush and curling iron she really couldn't do anything about that. Quickly, she got out of bed, slipped on her skirt and sweater. "Ready," she told him, not feeling ready at all.

With a glance over his shoulder, he beamed the flashlight out in the hall. "I have an oil lamp lit downstairs, but I don't want you to fall, so take your time. The steps are narrow."

Jed waited for her at the top of the stairs and descended slowly. She almost bumped into him when he stopped at the bottom. As he turned, his face was very close to hers. "Do you need anything before we get settled?"

I need to be held in your arms, she thought illogically, then dismissed the irrational longing. Jed was her boss! And hadn't she learned that getting close to anyone eventually hurt?

"No. I'm fine," she managed to answer. She could see the muscles under his T-shirt. Black hair curled in the vee. Awareness zipped between them, and she swallowed hard.

He cleared his throat and motioned toward the living room. "You take the sofa. I'll sleep in the recliner."

A blanket had been tossed on the sofa, along with a pillow. But she couldn't keep her eyes off of Jed as he sank into the recliner and raised the leg rest, stretching out his long limbs on top of it.

Wind blew against the house, causing the flames in the fireplace to crackle and leap. When Jed glanced at her, she made a point of pulling the blanket up and averting her gaze. The shadowed intimacy of the

room made them more aware of each other instead of
less. Brianne doubted if she was going to get any
sleep, but at least she'd be warm.

"Would you rather work for Dr. Olsen?" Jed's
deep voice carried an edge of tension.

"Because of what happened?"

The mantel clock ticked.

"Yes. I never should have kissed you. I don't want
you to feel uncomfortable. I can talk to Olsen about
it—"

"No. I don't want to work for another doctor. I
like working with you," she insisted quickly, in spite
of her own misgivings. She liked the way Jed handled
patients, and she was learning a lot from him.

The clock ticked loudly, marking off a few more
seconds.

"You're sure?"

"I'm very sure." Her fingers played with the satin
edge of the blanket and then she said, "Jed?"

"Yes?"

"Why did you leave a specialty practice to become
a general practitioner?" It was the most tactful way
she knew to pose the question. She wanted to know
why he'd gone to Alaska...and why he'd come back
here. She guessed something had driven him, and she
needed to know what it was.

"My reasons don't matter anymore. They're in the
past. I'm happy with what I'm doing now."

It was a polite way of telling her to mind her own
business. And she would...for tonight.

Chapter Three

Aware of the soft, restless sounds coming from the sofa, Jed shifted in the recliner, unable to let sleep overtake him. He was strung tighter than he'd ever been...ever since that kiss. Even running the snowblower on the walks, letting the icy wind and the cold wrap around him, hadn't diminished the effects from it. If he didn't block the memory from his mind, it replayed over and over. He wanted to take Brianne in his arms, do things with her he hadn't imagined since he'd had fantasies as a teenager.

With an effort, he pushed thoughts of her away and tried to replace them with pictures of an SUV he might buy. Unfortunately, he pictured Brianne in the SUV with him!

He blanked out the pictures the same way he did memories of Trisha, sealing them in a tight box he never willingly opened. But just as recollections of his daughter caught him unawares, just as a glance into a child's eyes stirred up emotions he never intended to feel again, he knew the passion and innocence and surrender of Brianne's kiss would gnaw at him until he acknowledged at least his physical need. Ever since the first moment he'd caught sight of her, his subconscious had let her slip into his dreams—her pretty face, the bouncy auburn curls shimmering like silk, that perfectly shaped mouth.

He reminded himself again that she was too young and he was too old...too old for that kind of involvement.

When he'd met his ex-wife, she'd seemed young and innocent, passionate and giving. It wasn't until after they were married that he'd learned Caroline had had an agenda. She'd been protected and safeguarded by her parents all her life, but she'd learned to manipulate them and everyone else to get what she wanted whether it was a new car or a husband she could mold into her version of the ideal.

Hadn't Brianne come from the same lifestyle? Had she been raised to believe her money and beauty could get her whatever she wanted? He'd been wrong about Caroline. Somehow she'd convinced him she was something she wasn't. Was Brianne as sweet and compassionate as she seemed? Even if she was, he was too cynical to believe she'd stay that way.

In the deep silence of the storm, the absence of the hum of the furnace magnified each and every one of the old house's sounds—the crackle of the fire, the rustle of Brianne's covers. Suddenly, though, her movements became more than a restless turning. In the glow of the fire, Jed could see her shaking her head back and forth.

Her hands came up in front of her as if she were

pushing something away. "No! No, you're wrong," she moaned. "It can't be Mom and Dad. It can't be."

The anguish in her voice tore at him. Jumping from the recliner, he quickly crossed the room and crouched by the sofa. "Brianne, wake up."

When she still seemed trapped by the nightmare, he said, "Brianne, it's Jed. You're safe. You're in my house. Wake up."

Finally, her eyes flew open. They were wide with sadness and wet with tears.

He'd been fooled by Caroline's tears too many times to count, but he knew these were different. Nightmare tears were genuine.

"I can't get the policeman's voice out of my head," Brianne murmured. "I remember every word. He described the accident, and I see it over and over again. I thought I was getting past it. I haven't had the dream for weeks."

Jed knew all about the kind of phone call Brianne had just dreamed about. He knew all about kindly officials who didn't know what to say or do when they were giving bad news and tried to make sense of something that couldn't possibly be real.

Taking Brianne's hand, he said, "It'll get better. If it's been a few weeks since your last nightmare, the next time might not be for a few months."

Almost angrily, she swung her legs to the floor. "Will it get better? I tell myself to grow up, to face reality, to accept the fact that my parents are gone. But my memories are so vivid. There are so many of them. They make me sad and yet...I want to hold on to them. Does that make any sense?"

It made perfect sense to him. Too well, he remembered how Trisha's black curls had dipped between her eyebrows. Too well, he remembered how her smile could make him feel higher than a kite. Too well, he remembered how her chubby little arms would come around his neck and he'd feel forty feet tall.

"Separating the memories from the grief takes time," he added, knowing it wasn't grief that haunted him now, but rather blame and guilt for not making sure his daughter had been kept safe. At first he'd blamed Caroline, who'd been spending the afternoon with Trisha instead of getting her nails manicured or her golf game honed which was how she usually spent her time while a nanny tended to Trisha. But not long after, he'd decided the fault was his own for leaving that weekend when their nanny had other plans.

"You sound as if you know all about it," Brianne noted softly.

Rising to his feet, he sat on the sofa beside her, fighting the urge to put his arm around her. Without giving anything away, he acknowledged, "I know about it."

After glancing at him, she fingered the pliant gold bracelet she always wore around her wrist. He'd noticed it before.

With her head bowed, her attention on the bracelet, she murmured, "My dad used to say, 'You can get over anything, Brianne. Life goes on so you have new opportunities to learn and to love.' Then he'd make us mugs of cocoa and somehow everything would seem better."

Shoulder to shoulder with Brianne, the top of her head not six inches from his nose and her creamy skin only a touch away, Jed felt the stirring of desire. From the memory she had just shared, he could tell how much she missed her father. The last thing he wanted to be was a father figure, or a mentor or even a colleague.

Physical need and Caroline's beauty had drawn him into a relationship with her. He wasn't about to let history repeat itself.

The fire popped. Brianne's gaze moved to the crackling logs. Jed used the small interruption as an excuse to end a conversation that had become too intimate, to end a night that had been too disconcerting.

Shifting away from her, he glanced out the window. "It's almost daybreak. I'd better split more firewood, since we don't know how long the electricity will be out."

She looked startled, as if his words weren't at all what she'd expected. Recovering, she nodded and smiled. "I'll rummage through the cupboards and see what I can come up with for breakfast."

He wanted to stay. He wanted to pull her into his arms and curl up on the sofa, nuzzle her neck and kiss those curved lips. Her smile made him forget how old he was and that there was wood to be split. It almost made him forget the vow he'd made to himself after he and Caroline had divorced...before he left for Alaska. He'd vowed that he would never take on responsibility for anyone else's happiness ever again.

That vow had been life-changing. Now he turned away from Brianne, stood and went to the kitchen for his coat. Physical exertion would help. If it didn't, he'd try something else.

* * *

Brianne had combed her hair as best she could with her fingers, and freshened up. She was opening a can of baked beans with an old-fashioned can opener she'd found in one of the drawers when Al came in, walking stiffly.

He wore a scowl until he saw her and then his expression brightened. "I must admit it's nice seeing a pretty face in my kitchen in the morning."

She laughed and accepted the compliment as genuine. She had a feeling Al never said something he didn't mean, and it was nice to be around someone like that. "I thought I'd warm up baked beans on the grate and try to make toast on the griddle. The fire's burned low enough that it shouldn't be too difficult."

"I'll take care of pulling things in and out so you don't get burned."

Al Sawyer was as chivalrous as he was old-fashioned, and she saw that same chivalry in Jed, whether he admitted it or not. He'd opened the door for her on more than one occasion, and he never took a seat unless she was seated first.

"That's fine with me," she told Al. "I put canned fruit out in the snow so it will be chilled when we want that, too."

"Does Jed know how inventive you are?"

She felt herself blush. "We haven't known each other very long. We've only worked together for a week."

"Hmm." After a few moments of silence, during which Brianne could feel Al studying her, he asked, "And just what do you think about my son?"

Keeping her hands busy, she took slices of bread from the plastic bag and set them on the griddle. "I don't know him very well."

"Jed doesn't make it easy to get to know him, especially since…" Al shut his mouth tight and then tried again. "That boy has always been complicated."

"In what way?" Brianne impulsively asked before she could stop herself.

Pulling out a chair with his booted foot, Al sank heavily onto it, then crossed his forearms on the table. "Did you know we're descended from the Sawyers who founded Sawyer Springs?"

"I wondered about that. Town history has it that they were adventurers but not very good at business. Was that true?"

"Sure was. Theodore Sawyer staked his claim here and established a town around Sawyer Lake with the friends and family he brought with him from the East. Old Teddy and his buddies decided a textile mill would bring prosperity to the town along with the farming."

Al shook his head. "The truth was he had no head for business! He established the textile mill, all right. People came from all around to find work. It employed over half the town. But then it went downhill. Teddy Sawyer couldn't cover his bills, and he couldn't pay his workers. So he sold out to a big honcho in New York. That guy only cared about the bottom line, not about the workers or the condition of the mill. Teddy's children inherited the money from the sale of the mill, and they squandered it. When they had nothing left, they took off for parts unknown. My own family, descended from Teddy's brother, had put down roots here. My father was a foreman at that mill and I became a foreman after him."

When Al paused, Brianne waited for more. Jed's father didn't disappoint her.

"I always made enough to get by. It was too much of a risk to move and hope I'd find something better someplace else. At least I had a job. Lots of men didn't. But the kids had to wear hand-me-downs," Al admitted. "We bought furniture at the second-hand shop and there was never anything extra. Jed grew up wanting more. He knew the history of the Sawyers, and he'd seen what they'd squandered. He pretended he didn't hear the jeers of the rich kids over in North Sawyer Springs, who wore fine clothes and had new bikes. Anything they wanted they got on a silver platter."

Brianne thought about all the advantages she'd had and how she'd never done anything to deserve them. When her parents had told her she was adopted, she'd felt as if she wasn't *really* a Barrington. It wasn't until after their death that she realized no parents could have loved her more than they had, and she *was* truly their daughter in all ways that mattered.

"I guess it was only natural for my kids to want more than I had," Al continued. "But Jed seemed to make it his mission to prove the Sawyers were worthy of being founding fathers. He was smart. Skipped the fifth grade. Finished college in three years instead of four and plowed into med school with scholarships, loans and grit. Actually, I don't think he wanted success for himself. He wanted to give his mother everything I could never give her. But she died before he got that fancy practice out in L.A. Then when his marriage fell apart..." Al gave a heavy sigh.

Brianne didn't want to keep anything from Al. "My family lived in North Sawyer Springs." She remembered now the way Jed had looked at her car. She'd been one of those kids who'd been handed everything on a silver platter. Did he believe the differences between them were too great to give them common ground? Or was something more than that going on, something that had to do with his life in L.A. and his divorce? Did she want to probe into it any further and become more involved?

Not if she knew what was good for her.

Before Al could say anything else, Jed swept into the kitchen, snow covered and ruddy cheeked. "The snow has almost stopped, and the plow has gone through once. I'm going to try and get to Beechwood after breakfast in case we have emergencies or appointments with folks who decide not to cancel. I'll take you home first," he said to Brianne.

But she shook her head, thinking about the patients who might come in. "You may need help. Especially if we have walk-ins. I'll go along with you."

"If you think you're going to be able to get your car going in this—"

"I know better than that," she said with a laugh. "It will sit in the parking lot until the roads are plowed and cindered."

After Jed glanced at the beans she'd poured into the pot and the slices of bread on the griddle, he asked, "Are you going to make toast in the fireplace? It's been years since I had that."

"I'll be careful not to burn it. I took a vacation on a dude ranch when I was sixteen. I learned a lot about cooking over campfires."

"Did you learn how to rope calves, too?" Al asked with a grin.

At the expression on Jed's face, she realized he'd

put distance between them again. It had probably been a mistake to mention the dude ranch, especially after what Al had told her. Her summer vacations, which included trips to Europe, pointed out even more effectively the differences in their backgrounds. Even if Jed had lived the high life as a plastic surgeon in L.A., he'd apparently decided a simple life—as he'd experienced in Deep River and here in Sawyer Springs—was better.

Keeping her voice lighthearted, she admitted, "I never quite got the hang of roping a calf, but I did learn how to bake bread and make biscuits. Turned out pie dough, too. I make a wicked apple pie."

Jed's eyebrows shot up. "And you still remember how to do all that?"

"I'll bring you a loaf of bread sometime," she said with a wink.

An hour later, just as they finished breakfast, the electricity came back on. Lights blazed, appliances hummed and the furnace puffed out heat. Jed had been cordial throughout the meal, yet he was guarded, and Brianne realized his father had been right. He was a difficult man to get to know.

Jed insisted Brianne let the dishes sit in the sink, that he'd do them later. He wanted to get to work to find out what appointments were canceled and who might be coming in. From everything she'd seen about him in the past week, she'd learned he was dedicated, cared about his patients and didn't treat them like numbers.

Beside Jed in his dad's truck, riding in silence, Brianne watched the last flakes of snow swirl down. Jed drove behind a plow, the cinders on the road shifting in its wake. Al's truck didn't have any problems with traction.

Brianne thought about last night, about how intimate it had seemed. The electricity being off had enhanced that. Firelight, candlelight and silence had made them even more aware of each other. But it had obviously been an intimacy Jed didn't want. She could see he intended to forget about their kiss, and she wished she could do the same.

Still, the conversation with Al had stoked her curiosity. What had happened to Jed in Los Angeles? Why had he taken a position in Alaska? Why had he come back to Sawyer Springs? Why would a plastic surgeon opt for a general practice?

She shouldn't care about Jed and his history and his life. He obviously wanted to keep their relationship professional—doctor and nurse. A man with secrets who found sharing difficult should be the last man to tempt her. How could she ever give herself to any man, when she knew that loving hurt? Love always seemed to end and leave a hole in your heart.

Yet she remembered her parents' marriage—how her dad had kissed her mom before he left the house, how her mom always waited up for him, how they never hesitated to hug or hold hands the rare times they had a chance to watch television together.

The silence in the cab of the truck had become almost stifling when Jed spotted a car by the side of the road, embedded in a snowbank. It was an older model and looked as if it had had its share of wear. A young woman who looked to be about Brianne's age was standing in front of it, gazing at the mound of snow as if she wished it would dissolve before her eyes.

"I'm going to stop," Jed decided, pulling up behind the vehicle.

"There are children in the car," Brianne noted.

Climbing out of the cab, Jed went around the side of the truck and took the snow shovel out of the back.

When Brianne rounded the fender a few moments later, the young woman was saying, "I skidded into the snowbank. I can't get out. It won't rock, and it won't go."

Brianne could see the young woman's coat wasn't heavy enough for the frigid weather, and she wasn't wearing gloves. Two children scrambled out of the car and came around to the front to join them.

Jed glanced at the kids and then examined the front right wheel. "I can get you out of here in a few minutes."

The boy, who looked to be about eight, peered up at Jed. "I can help."

The little girl, a red knit cap on her head smashing her brown hair, tugged on Jed's arm. "Me help, too." Brianne was just estimating that she must be about three when a paroxysm of coughing overtook the child.

Jed's expression became concerned, and Brianne could tell he didn't like the sound of that cough.

"I'm Ben," the little boy said. "That's Kimmie." Ben's upper lip was distorted, twisting his smile. He'd apparently had surgery for a cleft palate. Pointing to his sister, he added, "She's too little to help, and she's sick."

The woman held out her hand to Jed. "Doreen Steinmeyer." Glancing at Brianne, she included her when she added, "Thanks so much for stopping. I really don't want the kids out in this. Ben, Kimmie, get back in the car.''

"Oh, Mom," the boy wailed.

"Thanks for offering to help," Jed told the little boy, "but this will only take a few shovelfuls and your mom can drive away. Get back in the car and stay warm."

Once the children had complained a little more and their mother had herded them physically into the back seat, Jed approached the woman. "I don't like the sound of your daughter's cough. I'm a doctor at the Beechwood Family Practice. After I dig you out, why don't you follow me and bring her in? I'll check her over. Ben, too."

The young mother shook her head. "I can't do that. I don't have insurance. I lost my job two months ago and we certainly can't afford a doctor's bill."

"Don't worry about the fee," Jed stated firmly. "Just consider this part of the road service."

"But I have to pay you something."

"When you find work again, you can send me a payment. Now let me get the snow away from your wheels so we'll be on our way."

Ten minutes later they arrived, and Jed opened the door into the reception area. They all went inside. The offices were cold from the heat being off all night. The first thing Brianne did was check the thermostat to make sure it was set properly.

After they shed their coats, Jed took Doreen and her two children into an examination room. Brianne slipped in a few moments later to see if he needed help.

Dressed in a red flannel shirt and jeans and boots, Jed looked more like a woodsman than a physician.

But once he draped the stethoscope around his neck, he was all professional.

After he listened to the little boy's heart and lungs, he checked his ears, nose and throat. Then he did the same to Kimmie. As he checked her throat, using a tongue depressor, another coughing spell overtook her.

Jed laid his stethoscope on the counter and said, "I'll be right back."

Within a few minutes, he was giving instructions to Doreen, explaining how many times a day to use the cough medicine he'd found for Kimmie and how often to administer the antibiotic. "One pill a day for five days. They'll keep working for ten. If Kimmie still has a fever or her symptoms are worse, bring her back here after that. Understand?"

The woman's eyes filled with tears. "I don't know how to thank you."

"No thanks are necessary. This is what I do. It's why I'm here."

"The cost of the medicine…" she protested.

"Samples," Jed assured her. "We get lots of samples and I don't want them to go to waste."

Brianne knew they did get samples, but not for the particular antibiotic he'd given the woman for Kimmie.

After Doreen, Kimmie and Ben left, Jed went to the office and pulled out a form. He filled it in, then took out his wallet, slipping money and the form into the cash drawer. Brianne could see Jed wasn't bypassing procedure, and he was paying for the antibiotic himself.

Stepping into the office, she smiled. "That was nice of you."

Starting at her sudden presence, realizing she'd seen him put the cash in the drawer, he grew flushed. "Any doctor would have done the same."

"Maybe," Brianne acknowledged noncommittally. Tilting her head, she looked up at him. "Does Ben need further surgery?" She touched her lips, thinking about the little boy.

Jed's gaze went to her fingers, his voice husky. "Whoever did his surgery did an adequate job. But I could give Ben a perfect smile."

The last item Brianne had to settle in her parents' estate was an endowment. She had to decide on which charity to bestow it. She hadn't done that yet because she wanted to be sure she chose the best one. A fund for children like Ben might be a possibility.

Absently she removed her fingers from her lips, but she saw that Jed's gaze lingered there.

Was he remembering their kiss?

Spending the night under the same roof with him had made her more aware of everything about him, from the sweep of his black hair over his brow to the tiny scar by the side of his mouth. Kissing him had been an experience she'd never forget.

With all the questions bubbling up inside of her, all the feelings and sensations she'd never experienced before, she asked again, "Why did you give up plastic surgery for general medicine?"

When he stood, he seemed to fill the office. Yet Brianne didn't find his tall, muscular physique intimidating. In fact, quite the opposite.

After a moment, he said, "It's a long story."

Not knowing what had gotten into her, she didn't take the hint, but pursued the subject, anyway. "We don't have patients lined up in the waiting room, and I have time.''

"There might not be patients in the waiting room, but I have notes from yesterday that I need to dictate. Before we know it, we'll be getting calls and our afternoon patients will be backed up.''

Brianne had already checked the answering machine, to find all their morning appointments had canceled. Still, he was probably right about the afternoon.

When Jed moved toward the doorway, obviously not intending to tell her what she wanted to know, she started to move out of his way. But not quickly enough. They stood inches apart. Every sensation from the night before tangled around them—from their conversations in the dark to the touch of his lips on hers and that mind-boggling kiss.

For a moment, she thought he would kiss her again, but then he closed his eyes and took a deep breath. "I'm a private person, Brianne. I don't talk about my personal life and I don't talk about my past. There was no scandal attached to my leaving L.A., no malpractice suit, no mistake I might have been ashamed of, at least not in my medical practice. So why I left really doesn't concern you.''

"But..."

"You're too young to understand turning points. I had one. I came to a crossroads, and I had to make a decision whether to go straight ahead or to veer off and change my course and my life. I decided to veer off course. When you're old enough to realize—''

She was slow to anger, but his constant reference to her age lit a short fuse she didn't know she had. "Stop making me sound as if I'm a teenager who just bought her first training bra.''

Her comeback seemed to surprise him. Finally he muttered, "You're not far from it. We're not just talking age here, Brianne, we're talking experience. In another twenty years—"

"In another twenty years, I hope I won't be as arrogant and presumptuous as you are."

His brows arched. "Presumptuous and arrogant?"

She thought she heard a hint of amusement in his tone and that made her even more angry. "Yes, that's what I'd call it. But *you* might think you're being experienced and wise."

He shook his head. "More experienced than I want to be, and certainly not wise, or I would have been able to avoid this conversation. I think we should start over, Brianne, and wipe last night from the slate."

"Fine," she agreed, not knowing how she was going to do that. "Last night never happened. I never made breakfast over your fireplace, or slept on your sofa, or—"

The front door swung open. Lily and Janie burst inside.

Lily spotted them through the glass window and gave them a bright smile. "It looks as if you two survived the night."

Brianne had survived the night, all right. But if she knew what was good for her, she wouldn't question Jed again...because that was absolutely the way he wanted it!

Chapter Four

Brianne still didn't know what had gotten into her last week.

As she laid a patient folder on the receptionist's desk, she realized since she'd called Jed presumptuous and arrogant, whenever their gazes met, they both hurriedly found work to occupy them.

She was about to head to her office when the front door opened and Lily's daughter, Megan, ran inside followed by her grandmother. Bea Brinkman, Lily's mother, was a petite woman of five foot two, though a generous bosom and hips made her the look a bit like Santa Claus's wife. She even wore her gray hair tied up in a bun on the back of her head. Her quilted, three-quarter-length purple coat made her look even rounder and shorter.

A troubled expression was on her face as she hurried to the receptionist's window. Seeing Brianne, she motioned her over. They'd gotten to know each other since Brianne had moved in with Lily.

Megan scampered over to the corner where the box of toys was kept for their little patients, while Bea asked Brianne, "Is Lily free?"

"Is Megan all right?" Brianne replied.

"Oh yes, she's fine. We stopped at the house to pick up a few of her toys after kindergarten and... that's why I need to see Lily."

Brianne could see the worry creasing Bea's brow. "I'll check to see if she's free."

Lily had just gone into their shared office to fetch a can of soda when Brianne told her her mother was in the waiting room. Lily looked puzzled and then worried.

"Do you want me to come with you?" Brianne asked.

"Why don't you? You know Mom. She overdramatizes sometimes. If it's bad news, I might need you to keep Megan occupied."

Brianne nodded and followed her friend into the reception area. By that time, Jed was in the office talking to the receptionist about medical procedures he needed to have scheduled for a patient.

When Bea saw Lily, she said quickly, "You've got a problem. We set buckets in three different spots in your kitchen."

"Buckets?"

"Something's leaking. Not a gush, but a steady drip, drip, drip. You'll have to call someone before everything's ruined. If your father weren't out of town today, I'm sure he could tell you what to do. But he went to Madison to shop at that new hardware store. If he'd only let me get one of those cell phones, I could call him."

"Dad doesn't want another bill to pay every

month, and I can understand that," Lily said absently. "The leaks are probably coming from the melting snow on the porch roof. I really can't afford repairs this month. Maybe when I get home I can climb up there and shovel it off."

"Wipe that thought out of your head, Lily Brinkman Garrison," her mother ordered. "I won't have you crawling around on some roof, risking life and limb—"

From the corner of her eye, Brianne caught a movement in the office. A few moments later, Jed appeared beside her.

"Are you sure it's the roof, Lily?" he asked. "You could have ice melting under the siding."

Lily wrinkled her nose. "The porch roof should have been repaired and reshingled before winter, but I was hoping to make it through another season. I really wanted to knock out a wall upstairs to make Megan's bedroom larger instead of putting money into a roof, but now I can see that was probably foolish."

"I worked construction jobs when I was in high school and college. Would you like me to take a look at it?"

"A man who knows about these things," Bea said with a wide smile. "That's wonderful!" Turning to her daughter, she advised, "Maybe you should date a man who knows about something more than computers. You're Dr. Sawyer, aren't you? Lily told me all about you."

By now Lily was turning red, though Jed had apparently not taken offense. His eyes twinkled as he shook Mrs. Brinkman's hand. "Yes, I'm the new doctor here. Sometimes I wish I had a few of those computer skills. I've got a full roster until we close, and it will be dark when I leave here. Think you can manage with the buckets for tonight?'' he asked Lily and Brianne.

''It shouldn't be a problem as long as the leaks are just drips,'' Brianne answered, seeing that Lily was still embarrassed by what her mother had said.

When Jed's gaze caught Brianne's and held it for a few moments, she forgot about the roof and snow and an old Victorian house that needed a few repairs.

He cleared his throat and then spoke to the three women in general. ''Since the practice is closed on Thursdays, I can come over in the morning after hospital rounds.''

Although Sue and Janie worked six days a week, Lily and Brianne had off on both Thursday and Saturday. The doctors made hospital rounds as they did every day and rotated being on-call for the emergency room. Apparently Jed was willing to give up some of his free time for them.

''How's ten o'clock?'' Jed asked.

Lily nodded. ''That's fine. But are you sure you want to do this on your day off?''

He smiled at her. ''If I don't help with your roof, Dad'll try to convince me to join a poker game with his friends. They scalped me last week.''

For a moment, Brianne was surprised at the easy camaraderie Jed seemed to have with Lily. Maybe the two of them *should* be dating. After all, Lily was in her thirties.

But then Jed's gaze caught Brianne's again and tingles rippled up her spine. Maybe he wasn't comfortable with her, maybe she was trying to deny what she felt around him, because there *was* an attraction between them.

Every once in a while on Thursday morning Brianne quietly exited the back door of the Victorian to sneak a peek at Jed up on the porch roof. The bright winter sun beat down on him. Although the temperature was below freezing, he was hatless and his thick black hair gleamed. He was wearing a heavy, quilted plaid shirt and an insulated green vest, probably so he could move around easily. His long, jean-clad legs took him back and forth across the roof. He seemed surefooted, but she was afraid he'd fall.

Jed waved to Brianne. She thought she'd been unobtrusive in her comings and goings, but apparently he'd noticed.

"Tell Lily I'm almost finished," he called. "With the rotten wood replaced and the new shingles covering it, that should take care of the seepage from ice and snow melting. Before I come down, I want to make sure the siding up here doesn't have any gaps."

Brianne nodded and returned to the warmth of the kitchen.

At the sink, Lily was arranging cheese on a plate. "I asked him to stay for lunch. It was the least I could do."

"He said to tell you he's almost finished."

Brianne suddenly felt uncomfortable around Lily, as she had when they'd first met. Their friendship had developed slowly. Lily's invitation to move in with her had seemed like a practical solution for them both. Brianne's rent money would help Lily with the bills, and Lily and Megan would fill a void in Brianne's life with her parents gone. Still, she'd been cautious with Lily at first, but now considered her a real friend. Brianne didn't want to do anything to ruin that friendship. She wasn't quite sure how to go about posing the questions she wanted to ask.

At her silence, Lily cast her a curious glance. "Is something wrong? Are you uneasy having Jed here for lunch?"

"It's not that. I… Did you only ask him to thank him for fixing the roof?"

"Why else would I ask him?" Lily looked thoroughly puzzled.

"I thought maybe…you were interested in him."

Lily stopped arranging cheese slices on the plate. "I'm dating Doug."

"I know. But that started before Jed arrived, and once he came and after what your mom said yesterday, I thought you might be interested."

Lily laughed. "You know Mom, Brianne. In her mind I won't be happy until I have a husband again. She doesn't understand Doug's interest in computers, so I think she saw Jed as a better candidate. But that doesn't mean *I* do. In fact, Jed Sawyer's just not my type. Too much like my ex-husband. Part of him is shut tight with a lock and key. Behind that locked door there's a lot of intensity that I can't handle—don't want to handle. Doug is easygoing, doesn't have a thought he wouldn't share. Much more beta than alpha, and I like that."

Brianne already knew how intense Jed could be. Along with that intensity went a deep passion that almost scared her…maybe because she'd never experienced real passion. She'd never experienced being in love with a *man,* a man who could turn her to mush with a look. But she knew love always seemed to cause pain and if she could prevent herself from falling, she certainly would.

Carefully studying her now, Lily leaned against the counter and eyed her with concern. "Are you interested in Jed?"

She and Lily had had some frank discussions, but this one… "No. I mean…" Brianne sighed. "I don't want to be. But I feel so alive whenever he's around. I look at him and my heart races. That never happened with Bobby." Soon after she'd moved in, she'd told Lily all about Bobby.

"You and Bobby knew each other since you were kids. You were best friends. That's much different than just letting pheromones take over."

Brianne found herself smiling. "Is that what's happening? This is the result of pheromones?"

"I don't know, but I think you should be careful since Jed's been married and divorced. Do you know why he and his wife divorced?"

Brianne shook her head. "Do you?"

"No, but I think it's important for you to know before you decide to get involved. Whatever his marriage was or wasn't, it helped make him what he is now."

Brianne knew Lily's husband had cared more about work than his family, more about success than nurturing intimacy. He'd had affairs, and when Lily had found out, she'd known her marriage was over. Soon after the divorce, her husband had moved to Minneapolis, and now didn't even contact Megan. It was as if he'd wiped them out of his life.

All of this had made Lily strong. But her marriage had also made her wary of men who didn't talk easily, or who were too involved with their careers. The failure of her marriage had affected her deeply, and Brianne could see why she thought knowing about Jed's first marriage—if it was his first marriage— would be important.

Their conversation was interrupted when Megan ran into the kitchen, pulling her pink knit cap onto her head. "I dressed myself."

Megan had indeed dressed herself. Brianne could tell! Her snow pants were on backward. Her jacket was unzipped, her mittens hanging from the cuffs. Her boots were on the wrong feet.

Brianne could tell Lily was trying not to laugh as she commented, "I told her she could play outside in the snow for a little while before lunch. I guess she got tired of waiting for me to dress her. Come here, honey. You did a great job of dressing yourself, but we just have to make a couple of adjustments. Then you can go out."

Megan looked up at her mom. "Come out and play with me?"

"Oh, I can't right now. I'm getting lunch ready. Maybe Brianne will help you roll a snowman or a snow-woman."

"Sure I will. Let me get my coat and you can show me exactly where you want to put her."

Fifteen minutes later, Megan giggled as Brianne stuck tree branches in their snow-woman for arms. Megan had set her doll on the Adirondack chair on the back porch so Penelope could watch them play. Now the sound of the little girl's laughter was infectious, and Brianne felt almost as carefree as a kid again.

Movement by the porch caught her eye and she

raised her head. She saw Jed watching Megan, a terrifically sad expression on his face.

Brianne had caught a glimpse of that sadness before. Sometimes when he was treating children, she caught a flash of pain in his eyes. She knew he wouldn't talk about it. She knew he didn't want to discuss his past.

When she didn't look away fast enough, his gaze caught hers. She thought he'd turn away and disappear into the house, but instead he came toward them.

"Want to help?" Megan asked.

His eyes were so gentle as he gazed down on the little girl. "It looks as if it's almost finished."

Megan stared at the three balls of snow with the tree branches for arms. "She doesn't look real."

Jed laughed. "What do you think we can do about that?"

Megan's nose crinkled as she thought about it. "She needs a mouth and eyes and a nose."

"Why don't you go in and ask your mommy for a carrot and we'll use that for the nose," Brianne suggested. "Maybe Jed and I can find some stones for the eyes and mouth."

"And a scarf," Megan decided. "She needs clothes."

Jed murmured, "Can't have a naked snow-woman."

Brianne laughed as Megan ran to the porch, plucked Penelope from the chair and vanished inside.

She felt uncomfortable until Jed asked, "Does she take that doll everywhere?"

"Anywhere she can," Brianne answered with a smile.

"Is something about it special?"

He seemed to realize children latched on to specific toys for a reason. "I gave it to her. When I moved here, I had a few unpacked boxes I was going to store. As I was sorting through them, Megan saw Penelope and asked to hold her. It seemed a waste to keep the doll on a shelf or in a box when Megan was so taken with her."

"Was the doll a favorite keepsake?"

Remembering, Brianne smiled. "I took Penelope everywhere, too. My mom gave her to me when I was four. She'd gone out of town on business, and I missed her terribly. My dad must have told her. When she gave me the doll, she assured me whenever she was away, Penelope would watch over me."

After a few moments of silence, she changed the subject. "Lily told me you're staying for lunch."

"Lily's bound and determined to pay me back for the repairs. I told her I won't accept a check, so it looks like lunch is it."

Silence stretched between them again until Brianne finally broke it. "I'd better look for those stones for Megan. She'll want to put a smile on this lady before lunch." Taking off her insulated mittens, she stuffed them into her pocket. That's when she noticed her bracelet was gone.

"Oh, no." She fingered her wrist and immediately looked down at the snow-covered ground.

"What's wrong?"

"I lost my bracelet. It kept catching on the mitten cuff. The clasp must have come open. I've been meaning to get a safety put on..."

They both knew looking in the snow for a gold bracelet could be like looking for a needle in a haystack. Still, Jed immediately offered. "I'll help you look."

They canvassed the ground around the snow-woman in ever-widening circles, but Brianne had the hopeless feeling that their search was a lost cause. She *had* to find that bracelet. It was so important to her. It was her last link to her parents.

She wasn't even aware that tears were running down her cheeks until Jed caught her arm. "Brianne, it'll be okay. It's only a piece of jewelry."

She shook her head vehemently. "You don't understand. I have to find it. I just have to."

"All right," he said, looking puzzled but concerned. "You take the right side of the porch and I'll take the left. We'll go over every place you walked."

She usually checked for the bracelet every once in a while just to make sure it was still there. But in Megan's excitement over rolling the snow, Brianne had missed its disappearance.

After she'd scanned the ground inch by inch for a while, she caught sight of Jed standing by the porch, no longer looking on the ground.

He's given up, she thought.

She knew Jed had no idea what that bracelet meant to her. But she'd stay here looking all day if she had to. Maybe if she could borrow a metal detector from someone…

Suddenly Jed crossed to the left corner of the porch steps and stooped by the railing. A moment later, the sun gleamed off something gold in his hand.

Rushing over to him, she took the bracelet in her fingers, and couldn't help throwing her arms around Jed's neck and giving him a great big hug. "Thank you so much."

As he stood there holding her, her heart began racing. She wondered if his was, too, but then he pulled away and looked down at her. "You can thank the noon sun. I decided looking for the sparkle was easier than searching through the snow."

There was heat in his gaze that could have melted all the snow around them, but then he banked it and pulled farther away.

She dropped her arms from around his neck. The bracelet was clasped tight in her fingers and she opened her hand, looking at it nestled in her palm.

"May I see it?" he asked, gently taking it from her.

She nodded.

He examined the catch on the pliant gold links and then spotted the inscription. Obviously feeling he was invading her privacy, he didn't read it.

"Someone important gave this to you?"

"My parents. I found it when I was cleaning out Mom's dresser drawer. It was wrapped and a birthday card was attached. Mom was never a last-minute shopper. She had it ready and waiting for my birthday the following month."

Turning the bracelet on his hand, she could feel the calluses on his palm and wondered if they'd come from splitting firewood in Alaska, from building his own cabin or from whatever he did when he wasn't doctoring.

She showed him the inscription. "It says 'Always believe in tomorrow.' Just as my dad had his pat phrases, so did my mom. After we saw *Annie* she told me Always Believe in Tomorrow was a motto to live by."

All of a sudden Brianne did feel young and inexperienced and embarrassed by her deep feelings for her parents, for everything they had taught her, what all of it had meant to her.

Jed must have seen that. When she ducked her head, he put his thumb under her chin and lifted her face to his. "You had caring parents, Brianne. I understand that's something you never want to forget. That bracelet is a connection to your childhood and everything good about it."

Maybe he didn't want to share his past, but for some unfathomable reason she wanted him to understand hers. "It's not just that. When I was fourteen, I was doing a family tree project for school and I went through a box of papers in the attic. I discovered I was adopted. I found a P.I.'s report documenting who my mother was and how she died soon after she abandoned me. I confronted my parents with it and after that, I looked at them differently. I shouldn't have, but I did. It took me awhile to get a grip on all of it. And my relationship with my parents was never exactly the same. We got closer when I postponed college…" She stopped, not wanting to go into that, too. "It took their death," she continued, "going through all the pictures of our life together, finding this bracelet, for me to understand they *were* my real parents."

"That was a lot to handle as a kid. How did you get through it?"

Keeping the explanation simple, she admitted, "I had a good friend. And my parents kept reassuring me they loved me. But I never got the chance to tell them how grateful I was for everything they'd given me…everything they'd done for me."

In the silence of the sunny afternoon, she could see Jed absorbing everything she'd said. She wasn't exactly sure why it had seemed important to tell him. Maybe on some level she'd known he would understand.

Finally he confided, "During those long nights in Deep River, I had a lot of time to think. I left here chasing a life I thought I wanted. But I came back out of gratitude. My dad didn't have it any easier than we did when we were growing up. I thought if I could help him in some way now… But he doesn't seem to want my help—not financially, not physically, not any other way."

"Maybe he wants you to be in Sawyer Springs simply because you *want* to be in Sawyer Springs."

Jed shook his head. "All my life that was the opposite of what I wanted. I needed to escape from small-town living, small-town gossip, small-town expectations. Now I see life here in a different way. I still don't know if I'll stay. Especially if Dad keeps fighting me on everything I want to do for him. But I don't think of Sawyer Springs in resentful terms as I once did."

Thankful that Jed had just given her a puzzle piece of his life, too, Brianne was almost afraid to make a comment or ask a question. Before she could figure out what to say next, his face became guarded again and she knew he'd probably regret sharing his feelings with her.

Would she regret sharing hers with him? Sharing brought two people closer. How close did she want to get to her boss—to a man who made her heart leap at the sight of him? She kept reminding herself that loving someone always ended up hurting. Yet she'd seen how her parents had loved each other. She would never find that kind of commitment if she wasn't open to it.

Fingering the catch of her bracelet, Jed noted, "You'd better not wear this again until you get a safety chain put on it and have the clasp tightened."

They were back to being acquaintances again, and Brianne nodded, accepting Jed's withdrawal, in turmoil about letting her heart lead her into dangerous waters. "I'd better go in and see what's keeping Megan. She might be rooting in Lily's closet for her favorite dress to put on this snowlady."

"I'll load those old shingles into the back of Dad's truck. Tell Lily I'll be in shortly."

Then Jed was striding away from her as if they'd never had those moments of closeness.

Closing her fingers over the bracelet, Brianne mounted the steps and went inside.

The smell of the savory, rich soup cooking on the stove drew Jed's attention as he came in the Victorian's back door and shrugged off his vest. After he hung it around the back of a carved oak chair, he went to the stove to sniff appreciatively.

His stomach grumbled and he was glad to get his mind on another appetite other than the one Brianne always stirred up. When she'd hugged him, it had taken all his willpower not to pull her snug against him and kiss her even more deeply than he had before. But he wasn't a teenager with raging hormones. He wasn't even a young male who put getting physical needs met on a par with other life goals. He knew physical satisfaction carried a high price whether in a marriage or in an affair. After the first few heated encounters had drawn him into a relationship with Caroline and a quick marriage, he'd realized she'd pretended passion. Sex in their marriage had become a ritualistic duty for her, and he'd known it. He'd finally figured out she wanted to mold him into the man she'd wanted him to be, a carbon copy of her father—rich, successful, making friends with all the right people.

Hearing footsteps, he derailed his train of thought.

With a smile Lily swept into the kitchen and came over to the stove. "I think I should at least owe you another meal for your help."

"Don't start again, Lily. It felt good to be doing something with my hands."

"You heal with your hands," she reminded him.

"You know what I mean. The soup smells good."

"I make it often during the winter." She moved to straighten a napkin by one of the plates on the table, and he felt her gaze on him.

"What?" he asked.

"I saw you with Brianne...outside."

"You mean when we were searching for her bracelet?"

"Afterward."

The soup bubbling on the stove was the only sound in the kitchen. "Say what you have to say, Lily."

"I just want to warn you that Brianne's vulnerable right now. She lost her family and she's like a ship without an anchor."

"You think I'd take advantage of that?"

"I hope not."

"Maybe Brianne shouldn't be your concern."

Lily's arched brows told him as well as her words that she wouldn't let him intimidate her. "Brianne *is* my concern because she's become like a sister since she moved in. I don't want to see her get hurt."

This afternoon he'd realized Brianne's childhood hadn't been the rosy one he'd imagined. These two women probably had confided in each other, and Lily must know Brianne's background, too.

Realizing Lily was the type of woman who protected people she cared about, he offered, "I think you misinterpreted what you saw outside. Brianne was just happy she'd found her bracelet. That hug...meant nothing." At least that's what he was trying to tell himself.

"As I said before, Brianne is vulnerable. But I think you see her as young and inexperienced, too. She has more substance than you know."

Megan came running into the kitchen then, tugging Brianne behind her. "Mommy, Brianne let me use her raspberry soap to wash my hands." Releasing Brianne, she ran forward, holding her hands up to Lily's nose. "Smell them. It's raspberry."

Lily smelled her daughter's hands and then smiled. "Maybe *I'll* have to get some so you want to wash your hands more often."

When they all took seats at the table, Jed couldn't keep his gaze from Brianne—the swing of her curls around her cheeks, her bright eyes, the aura of innocence that told him she was inexperienced with men.

He didn't want to hurt her, and he didn't want her to shake up his world. It had been shaken up enough and now he just wanted to put it in some kind of order. That didn't include a woman sixteen years younger, or an involvement he'd regret.

When Lily placed the bowl of soup before him, he thanked her. He'd be on his way as soon as he finished his soup. He'd keep himself busy enough to put Brianne Barrington out of his thoughts, his mind and his dreams.

Chapter Five

After lunch, Megan waved from her car seat as Lily drove her to her kindergarten class. Brianne had come outside to see them off, and Jed had, too.

Now they stood on the porch together, watching the car drive away. "You have a good friend in Lily," he said.

"I know. She and Megan have become my family. I guess I'm the kind of person who needs connections…even if I'm afraid to make them sometimes."

She was definitely afraid of her growing feelings for Jed and where they could lead. Wasn't she heading for heartache if she let her feelings for him deepen? Yet not long before graduation, when she was trying to decide what type of nursing position she wanted to pursue, her mother had advised her not only to follow her heart, but to follow her passion. Brianne hadn't been sure what her mom had meant. But whenever she stood anywhere near Jed, she felt something deep stir. Was that passion? Or simply man-woman attraction?

The problem was, even if she did decide to get involved, could she be enough for Jed? She'd never been with a man...

"Don't you have friends here from when you were growing up?" he asked, studying her.

"Not really. Most of them have taken jobs outside of Sawyer Springs. How about you? Do you have friends here?"

"A few. I've been meaning to look them up but just haven't had the time. I haven't stayed in touch with them, but Dad gave me the lowdown on what they're doing. A friend I played football with now owns a contracting business. Another buddy manages a Christmas tree farm."

"What about your brother and sister? Are you in touch with them?"

Jed shook his head. "Ellie usually sends a note in her Christmas card. Christopher calls about once a year."

"I always wanted a brother or a sister."

His scrutiny made her uncomfortable as he asked, "And you can't imagine *not* staying in touch?"

"Every family is different," she answered diplomatically.

Sliding a hand into his vest pocket, he turned toward her. "Actually, since I'm here now, I've been thinking about trying to get my brother and sister to fly in to see Dad. It's been years since we were all together under the same roof."

Although Brianne noticed the mailman approaching, she didn't let that distract her from her conversation with Jed. "How would your dad feel about all of you being here?"

"I'm not sure. I haven't decided yet whether to talk to him about it or just surprise him. I'm afraid he'll think it's a lot of expense and folderol—as he calls it—for nothing. But he's not getting any younger, and it just feels like the right thing to do."

The mailman came up the walk, smiled and said good-afternoon. Then he handed Brianne a legal-size envelope. Jed saw the return address from a national foundation that sponsored cancer research.

"I imagine you get a lot of that kind of thing, asking for donations."

"Yes, I do. And I'm taking them all seriously right now. I have to make a decision about an endowment my parents left."

His brows hiked up. "About where the money goes? They didn't specify?"

"No. They left that up to me."

"That's a big responsibility for someone so young."

Instead of becoming angry this time, she asked gently, "Do you think of yourself as old?"

He gave her a rueful smile. "No. Not old as in senior citizen."

"Well..." She hesitated, then went on. "I don't think of myself as young. I've worked with charities since I was a teenager, helping my mom. I've even written grants. I might not be as worldly-wise as you are, but I'm more mature than you give me credit for."

When he studied her this time, his expression told her he might be looking at her differently. "Maybe you're right." With a small smile he added, "Right now my experience is telling me you'd better go inside.''

She'd come out without a coat and she *was* getting cold. But something about being with Jed make her warm, and the Wisconsin winter almost felt like spring.

Before she could protest or admit he was right, Jed started down the steps. ''I'll see you at work tomorrow.'' With a lift of his hand, he strode toward his dad's truck, which was parked at the curb.

Brianne watched him drive away, just as she had Lily and Megan. When she thought about everything she and Jed had discussed today, her tummy flip-flopped. Whether she wanted to or not, she was getting to know Dr. Jed Sawyer. Apparently certain subjects weren't off-limits for him, and they'd somehow tumbled into those.

If she got to know Jed better, *was* she headed for heartache?

Jed spent the rest of the afternoon buying a vehicle—a black SUV. Once home, he took his dad out for a ride. Grudgingly, Al admitted the car seemed to handle well. Then, while his dad dozed in his favorite recliner, Jed did the laundry and eventually hung two of his dad's flannel shirts on hangers in his clothes closet. Since his father usually grabbed his laundry from the laundry room and took care of it himself, Jed hadn't been inside the closet since he'd been home.

He was about to close the closet door when he saw something in the corner that made him go still. It was a cane. Did his dad have a condition he wasn't telling him about?

Deciding to take the bull by the horns, he returned downstairs and stood by his father's recliner in the living room, the cane in his hand. "I found this up in your closet. How long have you needed it?"

"What were you doing in my closet?"

His father's voice was almost angry, as if Jed was prying into his life. "Nothing sinister. Just hanging up your shirts."

"I can hang my *own* shirts," Al grumbled, then waved at the cane in Jed's hand. "I had a bad spell with my hip last year. I was laid up for a few weeks. But it went away."

"Why didn't you tell me? I called every few weeks and you didn't say a thing."

"And just what were you supposed to do from Alaska? Would you have flown back here to nurse me?"

Jed wasn't sure what he would have done, but he hadn't been given the chance to find out. "Did Ellie and Chris know?"

"Of course not. Women from the church brought me my meals. My buddies brought me everything else I needed and kept me company. Why would I want you worrying about me?"

When Jed was silent, Al's voice softened a bit. "Look. I know you sank into a black hole after Trisha died, and you just wanted to disappear for a while. But don't blame me for not telling you about my life. You didn't tell me what was going on with you, either. Whenever I asked, everything was hunky-dory. Like hell it was. Do you think I didn't know that? Do you think I didn't worry?"

"I was fine," Jed insisted.

"Not at first. Not that first year, you weren't. But

I just rode it out. It was months between calls that year. Finally, when you went north, I figured out Alaska was giving you something you were looking for, even if it was just an escape. But coming back here now…'' Al shook his head. ''Don't think you're going to run my life. I do fine without you. When you leave again, I'll do fine then, too.''

Was his father telling the truth? Did he really have a network of people who helped him? Could he function on his own?

Whether his dad wanted him to run his life or not, Jed knew there was a suggestion he had to make. ''Maybe you don't want help. Maybe you don't need it in most cases. But there is something you *do* need, and that's a cleaning lady.''

Al almost came out of his chair. ''A cleaning lady? Somebody messing with my stuff? Moving it around so I can't find it? I'd have to clean up before she came! What's the point in that?''

Resistance was his dad's middle name, and Jed should have realized this idea would go over like a lead balloon. ''All right. If you won't let me hire a cleaning lady, then I'm going to have to do it myself. I hate cleaning, Dad, and I don't know what kind of job I'm going to do, but this place has a layer of dust that's three inches thick, and it isn't healthy. And I'll bet the floor in the kitchen hasn't seen a wet mop in years. That can't continue.''

''I hate the smell of those disinfectants and stuff.'' Al wrinkled his nose. ''They make me cough and sneeze.''

''I don't have to use them. I'll just get something antibacterial—orange or lemon.''

Al gripped the arms of his recliner. "You're set on interfering in my life, aren't you?"

"I'm set on keeping you healthy and making your life comfortable."

His father gave a frustrated shake of his head. "You do what you gotta do."

"Then you'll think about a cleaning lady? I could put a notice up at church."

"No cleaning lady."

"How about just once a month?" Jed cajoled.

"Once a month?" Al asked, thinking about it. "It depends on who she is. I don't want some female with her hat set for me coming in here. I don't want someone talking a blue streak, either. Or poking into my stuff. There'd be a list. She'd do what's on that list and nothing else."

That was a big concession. Despite his father's grumbles and gruffness, Jed knew his dad had to see the reality of his life.

"Think about making that list. I'm going to the store to buy cleaning supplies."

"I have one of those sponge mops. It's in the basement. I just don't like climbing those steps."

"You won't have to. Maybe we can make a place in the pantry for everything. Do you want to come along to the store?"

"No, I *don't* want to come along." Al aimed his remote control at the TV and switched the channel. "That show where they kick people off the island is on tonight. I'm not going to miss it."

Jed had to smile in spite of himself. His dad was an ornery old codger sometimes. But his idiosyncrasies made him lovable, too.

Fifteen minutes later, Jed was wandering the cleaning supplies aisle in the grocery store, thinking that if he flew his brother and sister in, it would definitely have to be a surprise, or his father would grouse from here till next year.

Jed studied the products on the shelves. He'd sounded as if he'd known what he was talking about when he told his father about antibacterial soaps. The truth was, he only knew what he'd heard or what he'd seen in advertisements on TV. The plethora of products was confusing. Would buying one of the mops with the prepackaged, wet refills be better than soap and a bucket and a squeegee?

"Looking for something special?" a soft voice asked.

When he turned, he gazed into Brianne's blue-green eyes and felt his insides lurch. She was dressed in a royal-blue wool jacket with a red knit scarf slung around her neck. Her red leggings matched the scarf, and he bet the outfit cost a bundle because the patch of embroidery on the jacket matched the same patch on the sides of her leggings. Caroline had worn similar designer suits when they'd gone skiing. Yet Brianne's pretty smile did things to him that Caroline's never had. On top of that, he'd seen a compassionate, caring side to Brianne he'd never even glimpsed in his ex-wife.

Moving away from the shelves, he shook his head. "Dad's house hasn't been cleaned well in the past few years. I decided to do the job. The truth is I don't know where to start. He doesn't like the smell of disinfectants."

Stepping forward, Brianne plucked a bottle of orange cleaner from the shelf. "This is a good one."

"You know about these things?"

She didn't take offense at the surprise in his voice, but simply shrugged. ''I didn't have a maid in college, you know. And since I moved in with Lily, we share the chores. Because of Megan, I know which products are safe and which ones aren't. Lily's picky about that.''

''Then there's the kitchen floor,'' Jed said, putting the cleaner into his cart.

''Did you say it's been awhile since it was scrubbed?''

''A *long* while.''

''You probably want a squeegee with a scrubber on the front. Just use a bucket with good old-fashioned detergent. A scrub brush might help for the tough spots. Are you going to do the whole house?''

''I'm going to try. Dad needs to have a cleaning lady come in, and he's thinking about that. It'll be hard, though, because he says he doesn't want a stranger messing with his things.''

''Is that so surprising?''

Jed laughed, realizing Brianne already knew his father fairly well. ''I guess not.''

''It sounds as if you could use help if you want to do this well. You'd be surprised how long it takes to really clean a place.''

''Are you offering?'' With a quick glance, he checked her hands and noted her nails were average length and painted the palest pink. Caroline had spent a couple of hours at the manicurist every week and had made emergency visits when she chipped one.

''I'd be glad to help. Lily and Megan are visiting her mother tonight. When they're not home, the house feels big and empty.''

Jed knew that feeling of emptiness well. After

Trisha was gone and Caroline had left, he'd sat in his den many nights listening to the silence. "Are you sure you want to start this tonight?"

"It's amazing what we could get done in a few hours."

"I'll let you help under one condition."

"What?"

"You let me take you to a restaurant in Madison for repayment. I saw a French bistro there that's supposed to be really good."

When he'd first spotted it, he'd thought about Brianne and how it was the kind of place she might be used to and like.

Although she hesitated a few moments, she finally said, "You've got a deal. Let's pick out a few more supplies and we can get started."

Standing on the porch while Jed opened the door, Brianne mentally kicked herself. If only Lily and Megan hadn't gone to Bea's tonight. If only Brianne hadn't decided to go grocery shopping. If only the exasperated, lost look on Jed's face as he'd studied the shelves of cleaning supplies hadn't urged her to leave loneliness in the Victorian and help him. Putting it all in perspective, she decided she really was just helping *Al* by cleaning his house.

When Jed crossed the threshold loaded with cleaning supplies, Brianne could hear Al begin to grumble. Then he saw Brianne. "Well, now. Jed didn't say you were going to be my cleaning lady. Are you?"

Setting one of the lighter bags on the chair—the only one Jed would let her carry—she took off her coat. "I told Jed I'd help. We'll finish twice as fast."

"Maybe this isn't going to be *too* bad. Where are

you going to start?'' Al asked, as Jed took his bags into the kitchen and shrugged out of his coat.

"The kitchen," Jed called back.

"The upstairs bathroom," Brianne said at the same time.

"I guess you'll stay out of each other's hair that way." Al's smile was wide.

"You can supervise," Brianne offered, knowing Al needed to feel as if he were involved, too. "You can tell me what you don't want to have disturbed. Is it all right if I air out those throw rugs in the hallway upstairs?" She remembered how well-trodden they'd looked.

"That's all right, I guess. Do you think airing them out is better than sweeping them?" Al asked seriously.

"We can do both. Do you mind if I take down the curtains?"

"You gonna put 'em back up again?"

Brianne suppressed a laugh. "Sure. If I get them into the washer quickly, they'll dry and be ready to iron before I leave."

"I doubt if my son's ever used an iron," Al confided in a mock whisper.

"I heard that," Jed called as he unpacked supplies. "I buy wrinkle-free shirts and if I take them out of the dryer soon enough, I don't need to iron them. Once in a while, though, I have to plug it in. You underestimate me, Dad."

Al's eyes narrowed as he cut his son a sharp glance. "I doubt that."

Crossing to the kitchen table, Brianne took the orange cleaner from the bag, a packet of reusable cloths as well as a canister of bathroom disinfectant wipes, and headed upstairs.

A half hour later, the curtains were spinning in the washing machine, the rugs hung over the porch banister and Brianne was almost ready to start the bathroom floor. Jed had bought two buckets, and she was using the smaller of those in the center of the floor. Cleaning was one of those chores she had to do, and she didn't like it any better than the next person. Yet she'd known Jed was right about the condition of Al's house. She'd seen the coating of dust on everything when she was there during the snowstorm.

Once more she told herself she'd volunteered to help because the two men had *needed* help. Yet Jed's invitation to dinner had thrown her into turmoil. Would he look on it as a date?

No. He was probably taking her to dinner outside of Sawyer Springs so there wouldn't be gossip. *She* shouldn't look at it as a date. The dinner would just be repayment for a favor, and if she remembered that, she could enjoy the night and not get caught up in…passion.

She heard Al's measured footsteps coming up the stairs, and then he was peeking around the corner into the bathroom. "Jed's scrubbing that kitchen floor like a madman. He's even down on his hands and knees."

"Sometimes that's the best way to do it."

"When Jed's determined, there's no stoppin' him."

There were so many facets to Jed, she couldn't help but ask, "Was he like that when he was a boy?"

"You betcha! I remember one summer he planted tomato plants—about fifteen of them. And they all came up."

"I'll bet his mother made lots of good things with them."

"Not exactly."

It was easy to see Al liked sharing his memories.

"She used some of them, but that wasn't what Jed grew them for," Al explained. "Every day, he'd go out with his wagon, selling them around the town. When I asked him what he was going to do with his money, I thought he was going to tell me it was for a new football or a catcher's mitt. But it wasn't. He wanted to buy his mama a silver hand mirror he'd seen in Madison for Christmas. He knew we couldn't afford things like that, and he wanted her to have something nice."

"I'm sure you're boring Brianne, Dad," said a voice from the hall.

Brianne had been so interested in what Al had to say that she hadn't heard Jed come up the stairs. "I'm not bored."

"She *likes* to listen to my yarns," Al said, pushing past his son and starting for the stairs.

As he watched his father slowly start down the narrow staircase, a worried look crossed Jed's face. Did Al have trouble on the stairs?

As soon as the older man was out of earshot, Jed asked Brianne, "Was your offer to help genuine, or did you just want to pry into my life? Did you figure if you couldn't get answers one way, you'd get them out of my dad?"

Jed's privacy was evidently a bone of contention between them. He thought her motives were anything but pristine. Her own self-talk about why she'd offered to help urged her to wonder about her motives, too. Maybe she just liked being near him. That gave her a jolt that disturbed her almost as much as his words.

Holding on to the temper he seemed to have lit again, she plopped the squeegee mop into the bucket, making the suds fly. "I offered to help because I thought you needed help. I didn't want you using furniture polish on the floor! And I *like* your dad. I think he's lonely. Listening isn't a hardship for me." That said, she ignored Jed, pulled the mop out of the bucket, squeezed it out and began swishing it back and forth.

Stepping into the bathroom, Jed gently clasped her arm.

"What?" she asked impatiently.

"I'm embarrassed by what my father told you."

She stilled. "Why? It's a wonderful story and a wonderful memory."

Jed shifted as if uncomfortable talking about it. "It wasn't something I made public. Dad was the only one who knew the real reason for selling the tomatoes."

The hum of the TV floated up to the second floor. Meeting Jed's gaze squarely, she asked, "Are you afraid someone might see that you're not the tough guy you pretend to be? It's admirable for a man to have a tender heart."

Releasing her arm, Jed took a few steps back. "Tender hearts are as vulnerable as idealistic ones."

She knew he thought he was wise and experienced and so much older than she was. She also knew he always tried to get the last word. This time it wasn't going to happen.

She pointed to his chest. "Your heart makes you who you are. I like that man I sometimes glimpse underneath the rough veneer. You shouldn't try so hard to push everyone away. If that's what you really want, you should have stayed in Alaska.''

After that spate of thoughts, she turned away from him and went back to scrubbing the floor. A few seconds later, she breathed a sigh of relief when she heard his footsteps on the stairs.

During the next couple of hours, while Brianne dusted and wiped, Jed moved furniture and vacuumed. When they passed each other, they kept moving. It was almost nine-thirty when she'd ironed the last of the curtains.

Jed came into the kitchen and watched her dump the water out of the steam iron. ''Dad's snoozing in his recliner. Don't feel as if you have to stay while I hang the curtains.''

It was obvious he was anxious to get rid of her. Maybe he was even sorry he had accepted her help. ''Look, Jed, about dinner… We don't have to go.''

''When I make a deal, I keep it. Are you free tomorrow night?''

He obviously wanted to fulfil his part of the bargain and get it over with. So be it. ''Yes, I'm free,'' she said quietly. ''Should I dress up?''

''I'll need to wear a suit and tie, if that's any indication.''

''It is.''

His gaze stayed on hers for a few long moments. ''I'll pick you up at seven.''

A few minutes later Brianne had donned her coat, said goodbye to Al and was on her way out the door. But this time Jed held her elbow and didn't let go. ''Thank you, Brianne. We do appreciate your help.''

His words were gentle, and they warmed her as she stepped outside into the cold night.

After Brianne left, Jed rehung the curtains. The house didn't only seem clean now, it seemed less musty. And with Brianne's touch in every room, turning a rug around here, straightening a picture on the wall there, it seemed less out-of-date. Less asleep.

A short time later, Al said good-night and went up to bed, his steps on the stairs halting. Was his hip bothering him again? Jed wondered. Or maybe arthritis was developing in his knees.

The telephone on the stand in the living room seemed to beckon to Jed. Taking out his wallet, he pulled out a slip of paper with two phone numbers. Then he sat and looked at the first. Maybe Ellie would be out for the evening. Maybe she'd be at one of the parties *he'd* started to recoil from during those last years with Caroline. There was only one way to find out.

He punched in the number and waited.

After two rings, his sister picked up the phone. "Hello. Ellie Sawyer here."

"Ellie, it's Jed."

There were a few moments of silence. "It's been awhile," she drawled, with that scolding sisterly tone.

"I know it has. I got your Christmas card."

"I guess you didn't send any?"

"Are you itching for a fight?" he asked.

He heard her sigh and then murmur, "No. But I tried to call you last week at that number in Alaska and they said you'd left. The person I talked to didn't know much of anything and didn't seem inclined to ask anyone. I've been worried."

"I'm sorry, Ellie. I've been meaning to call you. I'm at Dad's. I'm practicing medicine here now. I thought if you called him, he'd tell you."

Now it was her turn to sound sheepish. "I haven't called him since before Christmas. I've had so many projects to work on, so many meetings, a new—" She stopped suddenly. "We're a fine pair."

"And Chris? Have you heard from him lately?"

"Not since Thanksgiving. He was in L.A. for a conference and we went out to dinner."

"I know you're busy," Jed said sympathetically. "We're *all* busy. But I think it's time we put something more important first. Dad's not getting any younger and I thought it might be a good idea if we had a...reunion within the next few weeks if we could swing it."

"Is he sick?" She sounded disturbed by that thought.

"No. But it shouldn't have to come to that, should it?"

After a pause, she stated, "You're right. It shouldn't. Let me check my calendar."

He heard a rustling and then quiet pensiveness. Finally, she said, "It's tight, but I could get away in two weeks. Maybe for a four-day weekend. Fly in Thursday, out on Sunday. Are you going to call Chris?"

"Yes. I'll see what his schedule looks like and then I'll get back to you. I'll try to catch him tonight, but if I can't, will you be there tomorrow?"

"In the morning."

"Okay, morning it is."

"Jed, how are *you?*"

"Better," he said, realizing that he was. Since he'd come to Sawyer Springs his outlook had changed.

A little voice asked, *Did Brianne have something to do with that?*

He ignored the voice and listened as Ellie responded, "I'm glad you're better. Trisha's drowning was awful, but I knew you'd get beyond it. Has Sawyer Springs changed in the past few years?"

It had been that long since she'd been back. "Not a lot. They enlarged the mall, opened more movie theaters. There's another grocery store on the east end now. Basically, it's the same as when we grew up. I'm seeing it differently, though."

"Maybe I will, too. Are you thinking about staying?"

"I haven't decided yet. I'd better try to get Chris before it gets too late. He's on East Coast time."

"All right. Good night, Jed. I'll talk to you tomorrow."

"Tomorrow," he repeated.

What would it be like to spend a weekend under the same roof with his brother and sister again?

Maybe he'd have the chance to find out.

Chapter Six

The restaurant food had been wonderful, Brianne thought, as she rode beside Jed back to Sawyer Springs in his new SUV. They'd had a few awkward moments, mainly because of the vibrations zipping between them. Repeatedly, Brianne had tried to remember she was having dinner with her boss. Most of the evening, their conversation had centered on their work, Jed's dad, the old Victorian house she lived in and the town's penchant for ice-skating on Sawyer Lake.

Now Jed was silent as he drove, and Brianne wondered what he was thinking, if he had enjoyed the evening at all, or if it had been a simple payback.

As they entered the northern boundaries of Sawyer Springs, Brianne gestured toward the side streets. "That's my old neighborhood."

"What was the address?"

"Seven-fifty-one Barberry Circle."

"Do you want to drive past?"

She thought about it for a moment. "Yes, I'd like that. I haven't driven by since I sold it."

As soon as Jed turned down the street, she decided driving past her childhood home was a mistake. Her father had pulled her in a wagon on these streets when she was a toddler. On her bicycle she'd maneuvered around the tall maples, beeches and Fraser firs to visit friends. Granted, she hadn't spent much time here since she'd been away at college, but home was home. Yet when she thought about that, it didn't feel much like home anymore, either.

Most of the addresses were clearly illuminated by lights on posts, on sidewalks or spotlighted by overhead porch lamps. When they came to 751, Brianne spotted a heart-shaped grapevine wreath on the door. There was light throughout the first floor, and she noticed lacy curtains in the living room windows.

"Was it hard for you to sell it?" Jed asked.

"The hardest thing I've ever had to do. There were memories in every room, every corner. By selling it, I was afraid I wouldn't feel my parents' presence anywhere again."

"And have you?" His voice was deep and low, acknowledging the fact that his question might be a difficult one to answer.

"Yes, I've felt them. I know it might be silly to some people, but I feel as if they're angels watching over me." She suddenly felt embarrassed at the naive, even childish thought. Yet it was the truth.

Catching a quick glimpse of Jed's profile, she didn't notice any scorn on his face. In fact, he seemed to be thinking about what she'd said. "It would be nice to be able to believe that about the people we love."

"You can't?"

"I'm a doctor, remember? A man of science. It's hard for me to believe in something I can't see."

Suddenly he changed the subject, as if it made him uncomfortable. "When you were a teenager, what did you do on weekends with friends?"

"Sometimes a group of us went to the country club for dinner, dancing, just hanging around watching the big screen TV."

As soon as she said it, he started the car again. "I did the country club scene in L.A. But you know what? I had a whole lot more fun someplace else when I was a teenager. Would you like to see it?"

"Sure."

Making a right turn, Jed headed toward the east section of town. After a few more turns onto side streets, they passed a bar and a restaurant and finally pulled up in front of an old wooden building. From the glow of the streetlamps Brianne could tell it looked as if it needed a good coat of paint. The neon sign over the door was green: Joe's Pool Hall.

A few minutes later, Jed had parked and was guiding her inside. There was a short and battered wooden bar. Men and women sat before it, mostly drinking beer. Brianne definitely felt overdressed in her shantung teal sheath with its bolero jacket and matching high heels. But Jed didn't seem to think a thing about how they were dressed as he led her through the bar area into the main hall. There were at least six pool tables, a jukebox, a Foosball game and a row of pinball machines. Mounted fish trophies were interspersed with the picture of a man and his latest catch. She assumed he was the owner.

As Jed guided Brianne, his hand rested at the small

of her back. She seemed to feel its heat through the camel wool coat and the fabric of her dress, though she chided herself that that was impossible.

"Joe's owned this place since I was about seven," Jed explained. "I remember the first time Dad brought me in here."

"Uh-oh," she joked. "It sounds as if you might be an expert at pool."

"I might be. Wouldn't you rather have an expert teaching you how to play than an amateur?"

When she glanced up at him, his eyes sparkled with the enjoyment of being back in an old haunt.

"The closest I've ever been to a pool table is Ping-Pong."

Jed laughed. "Then it's time you had your first taste of it."

Finding two high-backed chrome-and-vinyl chairs by an empty table, he took off his suit coat and threw it over one of them. Then he loosened his tie, tossed that on top of the jacket and rolled up his sleeves.

He was so very sexy that she tingled all over just looking at him. He definitely seemed more relaxed than she'd ever seen him.

As she took off her coat and laid it on top of his, she realized with dismay that her attraction to Jed was growing rather than diminishing. She also realized she didn't merely feel attraction. Working beside him day after day for the past few weeks, she'd learned to respect and admire him, too.

After Jed racked the balls, he picked up a cue stick along the wall, chalked it and grinned over his shoulder at her. "Ready for your first lesson?"

It was a rhetorical question, but her heart rate speeded up as she stepped beside him and waited.

Jed taught her the basics, letting her try shot after shot. They both laughed when her ball careened crazily. She liked the deep, rich sound of his laughter.

When her ball missed its mark yet another time, he narrowed his eyes and came toward her. "Let me show you where to put your hands."

Suddenly he seemed to surround her as his arms encircled her, and she practically dropped the cue stick. His chest was against her shoulder, and she found herself breathing more rapidly, inhaling his cologne and feeling his warm breath brush her cheek.

"Like this," he instructed. Holding the cue stick together, they made the shot. The ball in their sights spun and then dropped into the hole.

"You make it seem easy," she whispered, almost breathless now.

His jaw rubbed her cheek. Or was it only her imagination?

Straightening, he remarked off-handedly, "It just takes practice."

"Maybe the little lady should take off her jacket," a male voice advised from behind them.

When they both turned toward their observer, Jed's face broke into a smile. "Rob! How are you doing? It's been awhile."

As the two men slapped each other on the back, Brianne wondered if this was one of the buddies Jed had told her about. Jed's friend was about five-ten and good-looking, with sandy-blond hair and blue eyes that looked at his friend in amusement. He was wearing jeans and a red football shirt.

"I heard a bear got you in Alaska," Rob drawled. "Never expected to see you back here again."

"Sawyer Springs must be in my blood. Or maybe it's all those football games I want to relive."

"We'll have to play a game of ice football on the lake while you're here," Rob suggested, with a wink at Brianne that told her he hadn't forgotten about her.

"Ice football?" Brianne asked curiously.

"You don't want to know," Jed responded with a grimace. "Some people ice-skate on the lake in winter. We played football. It was the way to get more battle scars."

"Women *love* battle scars," Rob assured Brianne with a straight face.

She couldn't help but laugh. That's when Rob asked Jed, "Well, aren't you going to introduce us? She's a lot prettier to look at when she's playing pool than you are."

Brianne felt herself flushing.

After introductions were made, Jed asked Rob, "Do you want to join us? We can cool our cue sticks and have a drink."

His friend thought about it for a moment. "Nope. Think I'll watch."

Jed gave him a suspicious look, but Rob just smiled, and Brianne knew she'd be even more nervous if both men were watching her.

Picking up the cue stick again, Jed murmured close to her ear, "Ignore him."

Actually, as she thought about it, she decided she probably could ignore Rob—but not Jed. Especially not when his arms went around her or his lips practically brushed her ear.

In spite of being a novice at the game, Brianne had fun and learned quickly as both men gave her pointers. Finally she and Jed actually played a game, with

Rob advising her. Once he came over beside her and pointed out the angle from which she should shoot. His cologne was heavier than Jed's, and nothing about his proximity made her pulse race. His winks and smiles were sheer flirting, and she saw a frown come over Jed's face once or twice. But the three of them laughed a lot and had a good time.

Jed won the game, of course, and Rob promised to order them a round of drinks. Wanting to freshen her lipstick and regroup, Brianne excused herself to go to the ladies' room.

After the men found a table in the bar area, Jed sat across from Rob, not altogether sure he liked this idea. He'd never intended tonight to be an actual date with Brianne. He'd intended to take her to dinner to thank her, and that was it. But somehow it had turned into more. He had to admit he was enjoying himself. At least he had been until Rob had come along and begun flirting with Brianne. Jed knew it was second nature to his buddy, and it had never bothered him before. Yet it did tonight.

"Is she from *the* Barrington family?" Rob asked, with a wave toward the ladies' room door.

"If you're asking if her father was Edward Barrington, yes he was."

"And her mother was Skyler Barrington? She came from money, too. Her parents owned a couple of hotels or something, didn't they?"

"Yes, they did."

Rob tilted his chair back on two legs. "Well, I guess you're in her league now, anyway, with that fancy practice you had in L.A. Couldn't believe it when I heard you went to Alaska. What were you thinking?"

"I was thinking my life needed a drastic change. You've always known what you wanted. It's taking me a while to figure it out."

Rob nodded. "I wanted to be a big fish in a small pond and I've done that. You, on the other hand, made a name for yourself in the big pond."

Changing the subject from *his* life, Jed said, "Dad told me you weren't married yet. Are you seeing anyone?" The question was as nonchalant as he could make it.

"No one in particular. I've been dating a college professor from Madison pretty regularly, but I don't think it's going anywhere." Rob gestured again toward the ladies' room door. "Are you trying to protect your turf?"

"Brianne isn't my turf. She works at Beechwood Family Practice with me. That's all."

"It didn't look that way when I came in and you two were huddled over that pool table."

"She's too young," Jed said dismissively, reminding himself of that fact once again.

"Is that it? Or are you using her age as an excuse not to get involved? Believe me, I can recognize the signs."

Was Rob right? Was he using Brianne's age as a reinforcing reason not to get entangled with a woman again? He still remembered the nights that he and Caroline had lain on separate sides of the bed, as if there was a giant barrier between them. Jed was sure if they hadn't had Trisha, their marriage would have disintegrated sooner than it had.

Possibly Rob's observation was on the mark and he was using Brianne's age as an excuse to cool his desire. He had enough on his plate with his practice and his father.

Still, as Brianne returned to the table, he felt his reaction to her in every atom of his being. Tonight he'd felt...happy, for the first time in a while.

Brianne ordered wine, while the two men settled on beers. For the next hour she heard stories of their football glory days. With her attention focused on them, she seemed absolutely absorbed. Jed realized that was one way she was very different from Caroline. His ex-wife always needed to be the center of attention. Brianne didn't. She was a good listener, and that was one of the reasons why she was a good nurse. She often put notes in patients' files that were perceptive *because* she listened well.

When Jed checked his watch and saw that it was after midnight, he asked Brianne if she was ready to leave. She said she was.

As they bade Rob goodbye and walked toward Jed's car, she said, "I had a good time tonight."

"You mean learning how to play pool?" he teased.

"That, and getting to know your friend. Did you really share a motorcycle when you were in high school?"

"Yep. Found an ad in the paper and decided to pool our money. One week it was mine, the next week it was his."

"Rob has his own contracting firm now?"

In spite of himself, Jed didn't like the note of interest in her voice. "We worked on the same construction crews in the summer. Building fascinated Rob, and once he'd put enough money together, he started his own company."

Jed walked her around to her side of the car and

opened the door. When she was inside, he rounded the hood and climbed in the driver's side.

After they'd fastened their seat belts, he warned her, "He's not your type."

Rather than looking offended, she smiled slightly. Under the parking lot lights he could see she was curious as she asked, "Just what *is* my type?"

After he thought about it, he shrugged. "An investment banker."

Brianne burst out laughing. "I'd probably be bored to tears with an investment banker. From what I hear, they work long hours and have a passion for numbers."

Jed didn't ask where Brianne thought a man's passion should lie. That would get him into deep, deep waters.

After he started the car and turned out of the bar's parking lot, he asked, "Why do you live with Lily rather than in a place of your own?" She could have bought any house in Sawyer Springs if she'd wanted it.

"Why are you staying with your dad?" she replied.

"Because I might be here only temporarily."

After a short pause, she answered him. "When I moved in with Lily, I didn't know how long I was going to stay. I guess I needed friendship and a place to belong more than I needed my own house."

As Jed thought about Brianne's sentiments, he realized that between striving and escaping, he'd never really taken the time to belong.

Ten minutes later, he pulled up in front of the Victorian house and steeled himself against walking Brianne to the door. All night he'd denied the urge to pull her into his arms and kiss her. He'd teased them both at the pool hall and had been rewarded with an ache that still hadn't gone away. But his dad had raised him to be a gentleman, and he wasn't about to let her walk up to that house alone.

Once they'd strolled to the porch, he noted only one small light was burning inside the entranceway. He could see it through the elongated foyer window in the door. "I guess Lily already turned in."

"I'm usually the night owl, prowling about the kitchen at midnight for a glass of milk or a bowl of cereal."

Immediately, the picture of Brianne in a nightgown entered his mind, and he thought about giving up the fight and hauling her into his arms. "Chamomile tea doesn't work for you?" he asked, remembering the advice she'd given him for his dad the first day they'd worked together.

"It does when I take the time to make it," she said with a smile. "Why is it we often resist the cure?"

When she smiled like that, a dimple appeared. The longing to kiss it was so strong he took a step back. He wished he knew the cure for his attraction to Brianne. He'd certainly make use of it.

"I'm not sure why we resist what we know is best for us. It must be human nature."

What was best for him now was a fast exit. Trying to forget what a good time he'd had tonight, he attempted to put the night back on track. "Thanks again for helping to clean Dad's house. We both appreciated it."

Brianne looked disconcerted for a moment, then recovered. "Give your dad my regards." A little awkwardly, she shrugged. "I'll see you on Monday."

Turning, she fitted her key into the lock and slipped inside the house.

When the door closed, Jed shoved his hands into his pockets and headed home, knowing he'd remember tonight for a long time to come.

Almost a week later, Jed and Brianne were coming out of a patient's exam room when Lily passed them in the hall. She said, "Corbin Dustoff just gave Janie a bunch of raffle tickets from the fire department. If you want any, they're on my desk. Oh, and Jed, you have a phone call. Dr. Davidson about Mr. Brown."

Brianne knew Jed had left a message for the cardiologist earlier in the morning and had been waiting for the return call.

He told Lily now, "My notes are out front. I'll take it there." Then he turned to Brianne. "Grab a twenty out of my wallet. It's in my suit coat jacket at my desk. Buy a few raffle tickets for me, will you?"

With a smile for both women, he hurried to the front desk.

"Busy morning," Lily remarked, as she walked with Brianne toward Jed's office.

"Yes, it is," Brianne said absently.

"Is he still treating you like a nurse rather than someone he took out on a date?"

The day after she and Jed had gone out, Brianne had admitted to Lily that she'd had a wonderful time. However, she'd explained Jed's parting comment had told her in no uncertain terms he'd simply been repaying a debt. Lily hadn't been so sure. However, Brianne's conclusion had been confirmed when, on Monday morning, Jed had resumed his professional demeanor with her and acted as if they'd never had dinner or shared drinks…or talked about things that mattered. Except when she glimpsed him watching her, or when she saw the flare of heat in his eyes and it stirred a like desire in her.

Now she responded to Lily's question. "I guess this is the way it's going to be."

Lily clasped Brianne's shoulder and gave it a squeeze, then hurried on to tend to Dr. Olsen's next patient.

Brianne ducked into Jed's office and saw his suit coat draped over the wooden desk chair. She felt for the bulge of his wallet and found it in the inside pocket. The wallet was a soft, black cowhide one that looked as if it had seen a few years of wear. She opened it, extracting a twenty dollar bill. Before she closed it, she got a glimpse of the plastic window where most men kept their driver's license. Jed's wasn't in evidence.

The picture that was there instead stopped Brianne abruptly, and she studied it. It was a photo of an adorable little girl of about three. She had black, curly hair and dancing green eyes. She was holding a stuffed dog that had only one ear, but Brianne could tell it was one of those favored, treasured toys…like her doll Penelope had been. The child was sitting on the grass, her legs crossed in front of her, the dog held against her Mickey Mouse T-shirt.

Who was this little girl? What did she mean to Jed?

All day long as Brianne worked with Jed, she wondered about the picture. Should she ask him about it? Had she invaded his privacy by looking at it?

No. He was the one who'd asked her to take money from his wallet. It wasn't as if she'd searched through it. Still…

It was almost five-thirty when Jed and Brianne finished with their last patient. Janie quickly did the billing and then left.

Lily waved on her way out and called, "Mom's sending lasagna with Megan, so we don't have to worry about cooking tonight."

Cooking was the last thing on Brianne's mind as she nodded to her friend and glimpsed Jed in his office, taking off his white coat and donning his suit jacket once more.

Crossing to the doorway, she motioned to his desk. "Did you get the raffle tickets?"

He patted his jacket pocket. "Safe and sound. What can I win?"

"A pontoon boat."

Jed laughed. "I don't know if I can make Dad a boat captain or not. He might get a kick out of it."

She hated to break the compatible if charged mood between them, but she had the feeling that picture was a key to Jed's attitude about a lot of things. "When I took the money from your wallet…"

Jed sobered as he made the connections in his mind and asked, "Yes?"

"I saw the picture of the little girl. She's adorable." Then Brianne made a stab in the dark. "Is she yours?"

He'd told her that his sister and brother didn't have any children, and she didn't know of another connection she could make.

"She *was* mine. She died four years ago."

As Brianne tried to absorb the shock of that, the telephone rang. The service picked up their calls after six, but it was only ten to the hour.

"I'll get it," Jed told her gruffly. It was clear he

didn't want to have a discussion with her about the picture she'd seen.

"Beechwood Family Practice," he answered.

As Brianne watched and listened, she saw his face become pale. "How serious is it? Okay. I'll be there in five minutes."

When he hung up the phone, Jed rubbed the back of his neck. "It's Dad. He fell down the basement steps. One of his friends found him there and called 911. They don't think anything's broken, but they're taking X rays. Dad's giving them a lot of guff, says he's perfectly fine. His blood pressure's up. I've got to get over there before he has a stroke."

Seeing Jed's worry, Brianne asked impulsively, "Would you like me to come along? Maybe I can calm him down a bit."

As Jed came closer to her, his gaze held hers and that heat appeared again. "I don't want to ruin your evening."

"If you don't want me there, Jed, it's fine. I just thought I might be able to help."

The electricity between them was potent enough that it crackled in the small office. They both seemed to hold their breath.

The heat in Jed's eye burned into a conflagration that troubled every part of her. They were both denying what they were feeling....

After interminable moments, Jed groaned and enfolded her in his arms. He pulled her close for an intense kiss.

Afterward, he set her away from him and gave a frustrated shake of his head. "Having you around is driving me nuts. I'm trying to keep distance between us for both our sakes."

Still breathless, she didn't know what to say.

Rubbing his hand up and down the back of his neck again, he finally concluded, "You probably can calm Dad down. He likes you. Seeing me will probably rile him more. If you want to come along, I'd be grateful."

Jed's kiss had stunned her in its intensity. Swallowing hard, she concentrated on what he'd said. Her heart felt incredibly light. For once in her adult life, she decided to forget about caution and follow her passion.

Smiling up at him, she said, "I'll get my coat."

Chapter Seven

The emergency room at Sawyer Springs General Hospital was bustling. When Jed inquired at the desk about where to find his father, a technician led them to a cubicle in the back.

Jed immediately spotted Ray Orndorff, one of Al's old cronies, by his bed. Ray's potbelly hung over his belt buckle, and he had his arms propped on it with his hands folded, as if he had nothing better to do than sit with an old friend and chew the fat.

But Al didn't look so calm. He glared at Ray now. "Why did you call him?"

Ray didn't flinch at his friend's tone. "Because I didn't know how serious this was. He's a doctor, Al. He can explain the medical mumbo jumbo they throw at us."

Al sniffed. "I'm fine. Don't worry about me." Then he spotted Brianne, who had come into the room behind Jed. His face brightened a little before he aimed his frustration with the whole situation at his son. "Did you need reinforcements?"

Jed had always found honesty to be the best route with his dad. "Yes, if you want to know the truth. I figured you'd be a cantankerous grouch who wouldn't let me help. Brianne seems to have a way with you."

As Al's face reddened, Jed wished this conversation had started off a little differently. Why did his father always make it so hard for him to help?

"Look, Dad. Brianne and I were finishing up at the office and she offered to come along. I didn't know if Ray could stay, and I thought Brianne could keep you company while I found out exactly what was wrong."

That seemed to mollify his father. Still, he grumbled, "Ray doesn't have any place better to go."

After Jed introduced Brianne to Ray, he moved toward the door. "I'll see what I can find out. Hold tight and maybe I can get you out of here before midnight."

In a matter of minutes, Jed found the orthopedic doctor on call, as well as the radiologist who was studying his father's x rays. Thank goodness, he hadn't broken anything.

The orthopedic physician returned to the cubicle with Jed. Brianne and Al were laughing as Ray related a story about walking to Al's house on snowshoes last winter when the roads were closed. The three of them quieted as the specialist crossed to the bed to discuss Al's condition with him.

He was Jed's age and smiled kindly at Al as the older man ordered, "Give it to me straight, Doc."

Dr. Ames chuckled. "Straight it is. You wrenched your knee. I want you to ice it, elevate it and stay off of it. If it's not better in a week, we'll do an MRI. We'll fit you with a knee brace and teach you how to use crutches.'' Taking a prescription from his pocket, he handed it to Al. "This will help the inflammation. Someone from PT will be here in a few minutes with the brace and crutches.''

After Dr. Ames left, Jed offered, "I'll find someone to cover my rounds tomorrow. That way you can stay off your feet and keep your knee iced and elevated.''

"You're not gonna stay home on *my* account.''

As the two men locked horns in a battle of wills, Ray stepped in. "Like Al said, I don't have anything to do. I'll come over tomorrow morning, Jed, and stay till you get back. I'm not a great cook, but I can fix sandwiches for lunch. Same with next week if Al still needs help.''

Since his wife died, Ray had too much time on his hands, Jed knew. He probably looked forward to doing a few things for his friend. Glancing from one man to the other, Jed asked, "Can I trust you two to stay out of trouble?''

"He got into trouble when I wasn't around,'' Ray joked.

"I'm sure that if your dad gives his word,'' Brianne interjected, "he'll keep it. And if he does, and he listens to the doctor's instructions, maybe I'll bake him bread sometime soon.''

Al grinned at her. "Homemade bread? I'll make sure I put my leg up and not move.''

They all laughed.

Moving to Ray's side, Jed clasped his shoulder. "Thanks for calling emergency services and notifying me.''

Ray looked a bit embarrassed and just shrugged. "That's what friends are for."

"Don't go all maudlin on me," Al grumbled. He looked up at Brianne. "You don't have to stick around and watch me make a fool of myself on crutches."

Brianne laid a gentle hand on his shoulder. "Take care of yourself." After a goodbye nod to Ray, she stepped outside the cubicle.

Jed joined her in the hall, remembering the conversation they'd had before they left Beechwood. His gut tightened once again. Had he subconsciously asked her to take that money out of his wallet, knowing she'd see Trisha's picture?

No.

It had simply been one of those coincidences that happened.

A nurse hurried by them and he was almost grateful for the activity. It made private conversation impossible. "Thanks for coming along," he said to Brianne now.

"I didn't do anything."

"Yes, you did. I saw the way my dad's eyes lit up when you came into the room. He was scared. You helped him deal with that fear."

"What I *did* was sidetrack him. It isn't hard to get Ray and your father to talk about their poker games or about Packers scores."

More and more often, Jed realized how Brianne almost belittled herself, how she didn't recognize her own accomplishments. Did that come from having two accomplished parents and needing to be perfect? From knowing she was adopted? "You have a gift with people, Brianne. I wish I had it."

"You do!" she protested. "You sincerely care about each one of your patients, and they feel that. Do you know how many doctors today don't have that gift?" She paused for a moment, then added, "I think it's always harder dealing with family than with anyone else. They expect you, as a medical professional, to have all the answers. You think your dad was less scared because I came? I saw the relief on his face because *you* were here. Don't underestimate the bond between the two of you, Jed. It's there. Maybe you're just too much alike to see it."

Wasn't that a thought! Jed chuckled. "Don't say that to my dad. He'd probably bar you from the house."

"He's proud of you, and you admire him, too. Maybe someday the two of you can tell each other what you really feel."

"I think you're wearing rose-colored glasses," he teased, unable to help himself. Sometimes he thought she was naive, but maybe she was just an extreme optimist.

After a quick look around, Brianne became very serious, and Jed braced himself for what he knew was coming.

"I'm sorry I noticed that picture in your wallet," she began. "I didn't intend to pry—"

"Didn't you?" He didn't ask the question unkindly, but she could have simply not mentioned seeing the picture.

Though she looked flustered for a moment, her chin came up and her eyes met his squarely. "No, I really didn't intend to pry. But when I saw that picture, a lot of things made sense. Sometimes when you're treating children, you look so sad."

How could she put her finger on it so easily? He'd believed he was a lot better than that at hiding what he was feeling.

A technician scurried past with a carrier of lab tubes, and Jed used the interruption to end the conversation. "Brianne, this isn't the place to talk about this—*if* I wanted to talk about it. I don't."

"Have you ever talked about it with anyone?" she pressed. "It might help."

"No. You find it easy to tell me how much you miss your parents. I'm not like that. And when a child dies…" He shook his head, as the ache in his chest became so great he couldn't even finish the thought.

Brianne reached out and clasped his forearm. "Jed, I'm sorry."

Stepping back, he pulled away from her—away from her youth and her innocence and her heartwarming sincerity. All of those were too much to deal with when he thought about Trisha. *Especially* when he thought about Trisha.

Why? Because Brianne would make an excellent mother?

Wherever that thought had come from, he pushed it into the deepest recesses of a forest where he never hiked anymore. "I'll walk you to your car."

"You don't have to do that."

"I want to see you safely inside it," Jed insisted, and wouldn't take no for an answer.

Their walk to Brianne's vehicle was a silent one. He guessed everything he'd said was still on her mind.

It never left his.

When she drove away moments later, he couldn't

help but wonder if Brianne might be right. Would talking about Trisha help him find peace of mind?

A long pass sailed into the very blue, end-of-January sky, and Jed almost lost it in the descending sun. With Ray and his dad engrossed in a checkers marathon, Al had insisted Jed find something to do Saturday afternoon and stop hovering. So when Rob had called…

Slipping over the ice, Jed knew he was nuts for playing football out here at his age, but it felt good to be tossing the ball again with Rob. Although they'd had a warmer than usual spell last week, it had snowed again last night—a good four inches.

Ready for the ball, Jed wasn't as prepared for the melted patch of snow. As soon as he caught the football, he skidded and ended up on his backside on the ice.

Rob came trotting over and offered him a hand up. ''Didn't I tell you this would be a blast?''

Jed laughed as he got to his feet. ''You just wanted a doctor around in case we hurt something.''

Rob laughed, too. ''I knew you had this afternoon off and I needed a couple of hours away from paperwork. I really need a vacation, but I just can't get away right now. This is the next best thing.''

Jed's gaze scanned the small lake. There were a few ice huts that fishermen invested in along the eastern edge. Fishermen who weren't as serious or who didn't want to go to that expense cut holes with ice augers when or where they could. To Jed's dismay, he thought he saw a fisherman using an ax toward the southern edge of the lake, where ice-skaters skated, mostly on weekends. He hoped the man's hole wouldn't exceed the twelve-inch limit. The warming trends they'd been having would make that area unsafe for skating if the ice didn't freeze as thick or as solid again.

Shouts of laughter reached them from about fifty yards from the lake where children were sledding down a slope into a field. Jed could see the shine of saucers and the flash of sleds as kids and adults alike enjoyed the sunny late afternoon.

After he checked his watch, Rob said, ''I'd better be getting back. The stack of paperwork isn't getting any shorter. What about you? Are you going to stay for the bonfire?''

Jed could see that a group of people who had apparently been sledding were going to start a fire at the edge of the lake. ''I might hike over there and watch the sledders for a while.''

Rob took the football from Jed. ''I'll hold on to this until we decide to play again.'' Then with a wave, he loped off, covering the ground almost as easily as he had when he was a running back heading for a touchdown.

Jed noticed there were more cars now in the parking area by the lake. Parents had brought their kids to take advantage of the good sledding conditions. Suddenly he recognized one of the cars. It was Lily Garrison's—he was sure of it. Moments later, as Lily got out and unfastened Megan from her car seat in the back, he saw Brianne exit the passenger side. All three were bundled up for sledding.

Confirming that fact, Lily and Brianne removed two sleds and a saucer from the trunk.

Without a second thought, Jed crossed to the trio as they approached the sledding area.

"Hi, Dr. Jed." Megan piped up right away.

"Hi, Megan. Just what are you going to do with that silver thing? Pull a snowman on it?"

She giggled. "No. I'm going to ride it down the hill. It's fun. Want to come?"

"I didn't bring a sled. It would be hard skidding down that hill on my jeans," he said, though they were already plenty damp from the snow and ice on the lake.

"We'd be glad to take turns with you," Lily offered with a smile.

Brianne teased, "I can always share my sled with Megan and you can try her saucer."

"You'd like to see that, wouldn't you?" he asked.

"You could prove to us you're not a stuffed shirt," she retorted with quick humor.

Lily took her daughter's hand and started walking to the top of the slope. "I'll leave that one alone."

When they were out of earshot, Jed asked Brianne, "Is that how you see me? As a stuffed shirt?"

Her answer was spontaneous. "No. But I think *you* see yourself that way sometimes. A little fun might do you a lot of good."

He'd had such a good time with Brianne at the pool hall. She brought a freshness into his life, a spirit of happiness he hadn't experienced in a very long time. Maybe she was right and he just had to let loose more often. It was funny, but now he felt as if he could.

"All right, Miss Smarty-pants Barrington." He took the rope of her sled in his hand. "Let's see who can make this sled go the farthest on this blanket of snow."

A few minutes later, trudging at his side, Brianne asked, "How's your dad?"

"Getting antsy. Thank goodness for Ray and his other buddies. After that brace comes off, I'd like to get Dad some physical therapy. Strengthening his back and leg muscles will help his knees."

"Do you think he'll go for that?"

"If he doesn't, maybe *you* can convince him."

"There's a limit even to what I can do."

When Jed saw her amused expression, he laughed.

A short time later he stood on the top of the hill with Brianne. It felt so good to breathe in the cold air that carried her perfume to him. She was dressed in a red ski suit with canary-yellow bands on the arms and across the front of the jacket. Her yellow hat came down over her forehead and covered her ears.

"Do you want to take the first run?" she asked him, nodding to the sled.

"No, you go first."

They took turns for a while, trying to beat each other's runs until the sun was almost slipping behind the horizon and the sled tracks became icy. Neither one of them bested the other because they guided the sled equally well. You couldn't grow up in Wisconsin and not take sledding seriously, Jed supposed.

When Brianne returned to the top of the hill for at least the tenth time, huffing and puffing now, Jed just grinned at her. "How about we take one last ride together? They've got the bonfire going and we might want to warm up a little before we go home. I think Megan and Lily already headed over."

"Sounds good to me. With more weight we can go faster and father."

"Aerodynamics at its best," Jed said with a chuckle, then motioned for her to sit on the sled first.

After she did, he realized what he'd suggested was

going to be more complicated than he'd anticipated. Lowering himself behind her, he stretched out a leg on either side of her, his jeans pressing against her hips and calves. When he reached around her for the guide, he knew the intimate contact was going to tease them both. Brianne felt so damn right against his body.

With his head bowed to hers, he asked near her ear, ''Are you ready?''

When she nodded, he used one booted foot to push them off, and soon they were flying down the hill, picking up speed. As the air rushed by them, Jed held Brianne tight. The world was a blur and he almost forgot the past he'd left, the future he'd been avoiding.

Then all at once their run was over. The sled ran out of speed, but his arms were still around her and he found his cheek next to hers. ''That was some ride.''

When she turned to look at him, her cheek grazed his jaw. ''It's a shame it's getting dark.''

The dusk was beginning to envelop them in purple shadows, and he thought about what it would be like to be with Brianne alone in the dark...in his bed.

The thought was so arousing, he slid back on the sled and then quickly stood. ''We'd better get to the bonfire before Lily sends out a search party.''

''She knows I'm with you. She knows I'm safe.'' Brianne stood, too, and her breath came almost as fast as his.

''Why do you think you're safe with me, Brianne?''

Hardly a heartbeat passed before she answered, ''I just know I am. You're a good man, Jed.''

"Even good men have their weaknesses," he confessed wryly, and lifted her chin, running his thumb over her cold cheek, which seemed to get warmer. When she shivered, he knew it wasn't from the cold. Whatever this chemistry was between them, it was powerful.

"Jed…" she began.

He shook his head because he knew she was going to ask something he didn't want to answer. "Not tonight, Brianne. Let's just keep it simple."

Then he wrapped his arm around her shoulders and they started up the hill.

When they reached the bonfire, Lily gave each of them a cup of hot chocolate someone had brought in a huge thermos. As they sipped and watched the flames, Jed saw Brianne's gaze shift to two teenage boys who had a hockey puck and sticks and were batting the puck to each other in the flickering light of the fire.

"They look as if they're having a good time." He remembered his hour with Rob on the ice, and it brought back their high school days together.

"They remind me of someone I knew who wanted to make a career of ice hockey."

Something in her voice alerted Jed and he asked, "Somebody important?"

"A childhood friend."

"Maybe more than a friend?" he prodded.

"I thought I was going to marry Bobby Spivak. We met each other in kindergarten and went all through school together. We were best friends and then…more than that."

Curious now, Jed asked, "Did he go off to play hockey and leave you behind?"

''No, he died and left me behind.''

Brianne had said it lightly, but he suddenly realized what it meant. She'd been abandoned by her mother, had lost her parents and someone else very close to her, too.

''Bobby's the reason I became a nurse,'' she said softly, her words a burst of white vapor. ''When we were seventeen, he had a fall on the ice. Because of severe bruising the doctor did bloodwork and discovered he had leukemia. I postponed college to spend time with him—go with him to chemo, play cards, read. We'd always talked about everything under the sun and we had time for that, too. But it was still so sudden.'' She gave a little shrug and it was eloquent because of everything she hadn't said.

''Bobby was the best friend who helped you after you learned you were adopted?''

She nodded.

Just when Jed thought he had Brianne figured out, he saw another facet of her. She'd had to mature beyond her years from the time she was fourteen. She had known sadness and grief and loss, just as he had.

In a flurry of childhood enthusiasm, Megan ran over to Brianne and tugged on her mittened hand. ''Mommy said Penelope's getting lonely for me in the car and we have to go.''

''Tell your mom I'll gather up my sled and meet her at the car.''

''I'll carry it over for you,'' Jed offered.

Her serious expression was replaced by a smile. ''I can drag it behind me, even after a day of sledding. I'm a lot stronger than I look.''

Brianne was trying to send him a message, and

he got it: she was a strong woman no matter what her age.

He'd said he wanted to keep things simple today. But his feelings for her were becoming too complicated. He suddenly realized he didn't just desire Brianne Barrington, he admired her and respected her, too. He also wanted to spend more time with her.

If he did, maybe he could tell her about Trisha.

It had been an odd week, Jed thought, as he finished rounds at the hospital. Every day he'd called from Beechwood during office hours to check on his father. He'd worked with Brianne as if he hadn't revealed something important to her. He'd remembered holding her close as they'd sped down the snowcovered hill. During all of that, he'd considered the idea of talking to her about Trisha, until it began to feel more comfortable. Driving home, he realized—he didn't know how to ease into the conversation.

When he walked in the door, his father said, "I'm going stir-crazy. I've gotta get out of here. Let's go bowling tomorrow night. I know I can't bowl, but at least I can watch the other guys have some fun. You can drop me off and one of them can—"

To ease into anything with Brianne, Jed had to be with her. "Maybe I'll ask Brianne to go along. She and I can bowl, too, and bring you home when you're ready."

"You think Brianne likes to bowl?"

"I don't know. But it won't hurt to ask." He remembered teaching her how to play pool, the feel of her body pressed close to his. However, tomorrow night wouldn't be about any of that. They'd simply have a relaxing time and then maybe…talk.

While his dad was finishing a quick supper of hot dogs and baked beans, Jed went to the living room to call Brianne. She answered the phone herself.

When he heard her voice, he couldn't help but smile. "Brianne, it's Jed."

"Is something wrong? Is your dad okay?"

"Dad's fine, just going stir-crazy. I told him I'd take him bowling tomorrow night. I was wondering if you'd like to come along?"

A few moments of silence had him holding his breath. Finally she said, "Saturday night the bowling alley is packed."

"I know. But Dad's league bowls at six. That's early for the evening crowd, and we should be able to get a lane. The restaurant there makes a great beef barbecue. We can bowl our own game, then eat and watch Dad's friends."

There was another hesitant pause. "People might talk if they see us together."

"I didn't hear any gossip about us playing pool...or sledding at the lake. Will it bother you if people talk?" he asked.

"I thought it might bother *you*. Isn't that why we went to Madison to dinner?"

"No," he said with a bit of force. "I took you there because I saw that restaurant and thought of you. It just seemed to be a place you'd like."

This time her silence told him she was surprised by that. "Did you think I didn't want to be seen with you?" he asked gently.

"You *are* my boss—"

"We work in the same practice together, Brianne. I don't put much store in what other people think— never have, never will. Now, if you don't want to go tomorrow night, I don't want you to feel obligated in any way.''

"I don't feel obligated. I *do* want to go. What time should I be ready?"

Jed felt inordinately pleased that Brianne had accepted his invitation...much too pleased for a bowling date!

Chapter Eight

The bowling alley was crowded. Jed stole a glance at Brianne as he held the door for his dad, who wasn't using crutches anymore, but was wearing his brace. When she passed through the door, too, Jed caught the scent of her perfume. Or was it the raspberry soap she used? Whatever it was, it tempted him to do more than talk to her.

Al saw his gang immediately, waved Jed away dismissively and headed toward the lanes. "See you later."

Brianne laughed. "I don't think we have to worry about him having a good time tonight."

"Just so he doesn't ignore the pain in his knee and try to bowl." Leading Brianne toward the counter where they could rent shoes, Jed remarked, "He's going to enjoy that bread. I think he thought you'd forget all about it."

"I don't forget promises," she said.

That simple statement brought Jed's gaze to hers.

He believed her. He knew even small promises were important, and Brianne seemed to understand that, too.

After they rented shoes, they crossed to the bench at the lanes with their score sheet. Brianne picked up a pencil, sat at the desk and wrote their names in the blanks.

Looking over her shoulder, she asked, "Did I happen to mention I was on the bowling team in college?"

Jed groaned. "And here I thought I'd run away with this."

"You did that at pool. I wasn't about to play a game with you again that I didn't have a good chance of winning."

He could tell she was teasing, and he guessed to her the fun was in the game. Her eyes took on a luminous sparkle as they both remembered how he'd taught her to hold the cue stick to make a shot. He had to remind himself that tonight wasn't about holding Brianne close or whispering something sweet in her ear.

However, as he watched her bowl—her lithe figure curvy and tempting in royal-blue leggings and a long sweater—he decided he didn't have to be close to her to want her, for his heart to race, for his imagination to go wild. He found himself marveling at the fact that the delight on her face when she made a strike was as arousing as the simple sight of her. She knew how to enjoy life, and he had forgotten how for years. In spite of fighting his constant attraction to her, he enjoyed working with her every day, spending time with her, feeling her compassion as she dealt with patients.

A few hours later, after they'd eaten and watched Al's friends finish their games, Jed drove home. His dad was in good spirits and talked about the goings-on with his buddies. The senior citizens club was planning a trip to the Wisconsin Dells this summer and he wanted to take it. Jed would champion that trip. Anything to keep his dad active and involved in life.

Since Al's house was closer to the bowling alley than Lily's Victorian, Jed had stopped there first. Now he asked Brianne, "Would you like to come in? I could light a fire and we could make hot chocolate."

"That sounds nice," she agreed softly.

Jed wasn't sure what he was doing or what he was going to say. Maybe they'd just drink the hot chocolate and not talk about anything important. But his gut had a churning feeling, and he knew tonight was about more than sitting in front of a cozy fire to keep warm.

After Al shucked off his coat, he headed for the stairs. "I'm beat. Jed, I'll see you in the morning. Brianne, thanks again for the bread. It probably won't last past tomorrow noon."

As Brianne slipped out of her coat and sat on the sofa, Al slowly took the steps one at a time.

Jed set a log on the fire and lit a match to the kindling. Glancing over his shoulder, he assured her, "It will get warmer in here in a few minutes."

"I'm fine. I heard the temperature's going to warm up again this week."

"I worry about the lake when that happens. Too much warmer weather and it won't be fit for skating."

As he took a seat on the sofa beside her, the mood

between them suddenly shifted. Small talk didn't seem to belong in the room.

"What's on your mind, Jed?" Brianne asked.

"I thought I was being so subtle." He forced a smile.

"You *were* subtle," she acknowledged. "But maybe I'm just getting to know you. You can't work with a person every day and not learn to understand what they're about."

Maybe that's why he felt close to Brianne—because they *did* work side by side every day. Yet when he thought about women he'd worked with in the past, he'd realized that a sense of closeness had never developed simply from working together.

Sitting forward on the sofa, he clasped his hands and dropped them between his knees. "I guess what you said has been on my mind."

"Talking about what happened to your daughter?"

Unclasping his hands, he rested them on his thighs, wondering why this was so damn hard. "Yeah. Whenever I think about Trisha I get this ache in my chest. I guess I never wanted to make it worse by talking about her."

"I don't think it works that way. I mean... sometimes it hurts to remember, but the telling of it somehow puts it into perspective."

With a sigh he admitted, "I've never had perspective on this. Maybe because of the guilt. I have so much to feel guilty about."

When Brianne didn't respond, but simply waited, he started with the easy part. "I told you I left Sawyer Springs to make a name for myself. I wanted to put my footprint on the world for everybody to see. Along with that, I wanted to make my parents' life comfortable. When I accepted the residency in Los Angeles, it was the perfect opportunity to do both. I chose plastic surgery, knowing I could make an exceptional living. I guess I didn't realize what I was getting into. I don't mean the plastic surgery itself. I loved the work. But the trappings that went with it, the differences in values, the differences in people…''

"Do you really think those differences are so great, Jed? Aren't people just people?''

Ever since he'd left L.A., he'd thought about that a lot. "I don't know. Maybe I just met the wrong ones. Maybe I just met the ones who didn't have meaning in their lives, and they looked at cars and success and women to put that meaning into it. I was looking for meaning when I met my ex-wife, Caroline.''

"Meaning?'' Brianne asked.

Once again she was showing him how perceptive she was. "All right. It didn't start out as meaning. Caroline played a great game of racquetball, and we paired up a few times. She was beautiful, charming, well-bred and *so* polished. I just never realized how polished.''

"You fell in love?''

Still staring into the fire, he said honestly, "I fell in lust. And then I fell for more than that. Her family seemed to have everything that I was striving for. Her father was the president of a bank. Her mother gave parties I had never seen the likes of before. And I've got to admit, along with the practice I'd become a part of, it all dazzled me. I began to see us having the perfect life…the perfect children. The first sign that we weren't meant to be together should have been our visit here, when she backed off from my dad and this house and wanted to stay in a hotel in Madison. I made excuses. Dad was gruff. He was rude. He wasn't well-educated. The house was a throwback to the fifties. Then Dad made it clear he didn't like Caroline. At the time, I just saw that as discord between him and me.''

He glanced at Brianne. ''I couldn't understand Dad's problem with Caroline until finally, after the first year of marriage, I realized he had seen a lot deeper than *I* had. Whereas I wanted to put meaning into my life and start a family, Caroline had her own agenda. She wanted to make me into her father. She wanted us to fly to Paris over a weekend to visit the Louvre…or ski in Vail with friends…or go shopping in New York City. I belonged to a group practice and except for once a month, weekends were my own. But I didn't want to spend them flying around the world. I wanted to have kids, play ball with my son, teach my daughter how to swim.'' At that, he felt the choking in his throat and stopped.

''Tell me about it,'' Brianne suggested softly.

Never before putting it into words, Jed found he needed a few moments to sort through it all. ''My marriage to Caroline was a shell. When she found out she was pregnant… It was an accident, because she was taking birth control pills. Still, she seemed to get used to the idea and liked the concept of having a baby. The only thing was she didn't want to be tied down by one, and insisted we hire a nanny. We compromised. She had help daily, Monday through Friday, but the nights and weekends were ours. I could tell she didn't like being trapped on the weekends. Often I'd take care of Trisha while Caroline played her tennis matches or went to Vail skiing. Once in a while, though, I had weekend commitments, too. When Trisha was barely three I had plans to speak at a conference in San Diego. I told Caroline that if she wanted the nanny to stay for the weekend, to hire her for those extra hours. But it turned out Mrs. Cunningham was busy and Caroline couldn't find anyone else. I think she intended to make a point of showing me how unhappy she was by staying with Trisha herself that weekend. I don't know.''

He couldn't look at Brianne now, and stared at the fire as the low flames licked at the log. ''I got a phone call on Saturday afternoon. It was the police. The officer told me my daughter had drowned.''

''Oh, Jed.''

If he didn't harden himself to the sympathy in Brianne's voice, he wouldn't be able to tell her the rest. ''I chartered a plane and flew home. The police were at the hospital with Caroline and her father. Apparently the gate on the fence around the pool hadn't been latched. Caroline said she'd only turned her back for a few minutes. But in those few minutes, Trisha had found her way into the pool and drowned. I hadn't taught her how to swim soon enough.'' His voice caught and he stopped, embarrassed that he didn't have better control of his emotions.

As Brianne eased forward on the sofa, her leg grazed his.

He swallowed a few times. ''The drowning was judged accidental. And it was. At first I wanted to keep my marriage together—it was all I had left. I told myself the same thing could have happened if I'd been home. But I knew that wasn't so. I watched

Trisha every moment, not because I had to, but because I wanted to."

Looking back, he recalled, "Caroline and I lived like strangers for a few months, until one night everything erupted. We had an argument that ended in her sobbing and blaming me for not being there that weekend. I was filled with rage against her for not being a good enough mother...until I realized she was right. If I had been home that weekend, Trisha would still be alive. We both realized that night that our marriage was over. Caroline moved out, and a month later, when I saw the notice that Deep River needed a doctor, I applied. I ran, escaped, disappeared into the snow and ice."

After a few pops as the fire consumed more of the logs, Brianne asked, "Did you find what you were looking for?"

"I found a life that was different. The practice was demanding in a primitive way, the hours longer than any place I'd worked. At the beginning, I just stayed numb. Then some part of me started coming alive again, and I saw the beauty of Alaska, the beauty in its people. I liked it there. But by the end of my stint, I realized I was still hiding. I needed to make decisions about where my life was going to go. Returning to Sawyer Springs was the first step."

The story might have ended there. The sharing might have stopped. But Brianne must have guessed he hadn't gone far enough because she asked, "What did you like the very best about being a daddy?"

Vividly then, he saw the many pictures of Trisha pass through his mind, and this time he didn't stop them. "I loved feeding her and watching her expressions change with the tastes. Each day was an adventure, because when she learned something new, I did, too. When I let myself, I remember so much. She had this way of sticking her two middle fingers into her mouth when she fell asleep. At night I'd go in and put my hand on her back to make sure she was breathing.'' He shook his head. ''It hurts so damn much, Brianne. Four years haven't changed a thing.''

When he turned his head, he met Brianne's gaze. Her eyes were moist, and he knew she understood a little bit of what he was saying. At that moment, he realized he didn't want her empathy, though.

All he wanted to do was get rid of the pain. All he wanted to do was make it vanish for a few minutes. It vanished whenever he kissed Brianne. Her taste and touch and sweetness always consumed him, and there was never room for anything else.

He needed to be consumed now.

When he leaned toward her, she hesitated only a moment and then lifted her face to his. With the kiss, he became immersed in everything he was trying to escape. Tonight he didn't try to control his hunger or the need of his body.

Holding Brianne's face between his hands, he kissed her long and hard and deep, until her hands went into his hair and her fingers clenched ferociously. When he broke the kiss, her lips clung to his and he almost went back for more.

But then she murmured his name.

Her voice was so soft...so filled with need. And he knew he'd done the wrong thing tonight. He knew it had been a mistake to bring her home and tell her anything.

''Brianne, are you a virgin?''

Her eyes fluttered open. ''Yes,'' she whispered.

Swearing, he moved a good six inches away from her. "We can't do this."

"Because I'm not experienced enough?"

"Because *I'm* sixteen years older than you. Because you don't know the first thing about passion between a man and a woman and what it can do. Because I never intend to get seriously involved again. Marriage costs too much."

As she absorbed his words, he saw reality sink in. If she wanted more than a one-night stand, she wasn't going to find it with him.

Her cheeks, which had been flushed from his kisses, now reddened even more. She looked away from him into the fire, and he could only imagine what she thought of him now.

"You'd better take me home," she said in a small voice.

That was exactly what he was going to do. Then he was going to figure out how to switch nurses with Dr. Olsen. Working with Brianne was too much of a distraction, and Jed wasn't about to make another mistake.

Brianne went through the motions of her job mechanically the following week. After Saturday night, she understood Jed's defenses better. She knew words wouldn't convince him to take a chance on love again. She wasn't exactly sure when she'd decided *she* should. All she knew was that her feelings for Jed had invaded and captured her. The problem was he'd obviously experienced only pain from his marriage. Nothing she could say or do would change that. Somehow she had to work with him, yet keep herself removed personally. It seemed an impossible task.

Fleetingly, she thought about the position she'd applied for on the team for Project Voyage, which traveled the world helping underprivileged children. Maybe she should check on her application and find out its status. Even if she *was* accepted, before she could leave Sawyer Springs, she still had a responsibility to her parents that she hadn't satisfied—their bequest.

The more she'd thought about it during the past few days, the more a plan had formed in her mind. The plan included Jed, but only because he was the most qualified to carry it out. Not only was he the most qualified, but what she could offer him might help him heal from the past.

He was dictating patient notes Wednesday afternoon when she rapped on his office door. As he looked up, she could see in his eyes the memory of everything that had happened between them on Saturday night. But she had to put that behind her. She had to go on with her life no matter what Jed did with his. If he refused her offer, she'd find someone else.

"May I talk to you for a few minutes?"

He pushed the off button on his tape recorder. "What is it?" he asked in a neutral tone.

That's how he'd been with her for three days— neutral—and she'd tried to be the same with him.

Stepping into the office, she sat in the chair beside his desk. Before Saturday night, she might have asked him if he was skipping lunch to work, but now small talk seemed to have no place between them. So she got right to the point.

"I've made a decision about my parents' bequest."

His brows arched as if he wondered what that had to do with him.

"I've been considering an idea ever since that day we stopped to help Doreen and her kids."

"Doreen has something to do with the bequest?"

"It's possible Ben could be the first recipient. What if I used my parents' endowment for a children's center for reconstructive surgery?"

He thought about it. "You'd want to set that up in Sawyer Springs?"

"Why not? Besides being good for children, it might give a boost to the town. People could bring their kids here from all over the United States. Beside the center, we could set up a house where they could stay while they're here, staffed by volunteers."

"We?"

"I'd like you to be the director, the force behind the center. You'd know exactly what it would need, what the kids would need, what the staff would need."

"Why me?" His tone was even and his face showed no emotion.

"Because I believe you would be perfect in the director's position."

"Brianne, I think Saturday night showed us that we have to be careful working together. I thought about going to Dr. Olsen and having you and Lily switch positions."

"You aren't satisfied with my work?"

"You know that's not it." His voice went deep and low. "We're attracted to each other and that makes for an uncomfortable situation. But I didn't want to discuss this with Dr. Olsen without talking to you about it first."

She knew it might be easier for her to work with Dr. Olsen, yet she liked working with Jed in spite of the tension between them. Even if she worked for Dr. Olsen, she'd still have contact with Jed and see him daily. She and Lily often helped both doctors. "Haven't we worked together perfectly well the past few days?" she asked softly.

After he considered it, he nodded. "We have."

"Then I'd like to continue working with you. And as far as the position with the reconstructive surgery center…that doesn't have to have anything to do with me."

"You hold the purse strings."

"That's true. But I can set up a board that doesn't include me. You can even select members. You'd be good at this, Jed. A project this size needs a force behind it to keep on track, to keep it moving. You could be that force. You can determine which children would need this type of surgery most."

His penetrating gaze wouldn't leave hers. "What's the *real* reason you're pressing for me to do this?"

Sometimes Jed's ability to see right through her disconcerted her. "I think you *need* to do it."

He was silent for a long time. Finally he insisted, "Just because you believe a position such as you're suggesting would be therapeutic for me doesn't mean it would be. Getting over a loss isn't as easy as throwing myself into work that matters."

"I know that. But don't you think it's something to think about?"

"How long do I have to make a decision?"

"There isn't a time limit. The money's invested and earning dividends. I just need to know one way or the other when you come to a decision, because I'm going to go ahead with the center whether you decide to direct it or not."

"This isn't a decision I'm going to make lightly. It could take some time."

"I understand that." Rising to her feet, she was afraid the days of personal conversation between them were over and now all they'd have would be a working relationship. Could she live with that? Was she holding on to that thread, hoping for more?

Crossing to the door, she stopped when Jed called her name.

"Are you sure you don't want to work for Dr. Olsen instead of me?"

"I'm sure," she decided without even having to think about it again. "You're a good doctor, Jed. I learn from you every day. As long as you find my work satisfactory, I'd like to continue being your nurse."

And then she left his office before tears came to her eyes…because she did want to be so much more.

When Bea Brinkman called Brianne to invite her to Lily's surprise party on Saturday, Brianne was happy to have something else to think about beside Jed. No matter how hard she tried, she couldn't evict him from her thoughts. Thank goodness Bea was sticking to balloons and crepe paper for decorations, rather than Valentine's Day hearts. To Brianne's dismay, Janie had hung Cupids from the ceiling in the reception area and main office! If only true love was as simple as hearts and flowers and happy little cherubs.

When Lily's mom asked Brianne for the names and numbers of everyone at Beechwood, Brianne made the list, wondering if Jed would go to the party. Part of her hoped he would. Part of her hoped he wouldn't.

When she offered to help Bea and Charlie Brinkman with the party, Bea asked her to pick up the helium balloons and the cake and bring them along on Saturday night. Brianne knew she could make some excuse for going out that evening and Lily wouldn't be any the wiser.

As soon as Brianne rushed into Bea's house Saturday evening, she was aware that Jed was already there. He was talking to Doug and Dr. Olsen and gave Brianne a nod of recognition. But his cool demeanor belied the sparks of desire in his eyes. Brianne could feel those sparks with her whole being. They were both fighting this attraction tooth and nail for very logical reasons. For very safe reasons…

She'd taken the safe route for years, keeping men at arm's length, preferring to spend time alone rather than entering the dating scene. Over and over she thought about the danger Jed posed to her heart, her fear that she could never be enough for a man like him, her fear he'd never heal from his marriage and loss of Trisha. She realized now the love she'd had for Bobby had been true—they'd had a bond that went beyond friendship and went beyond his death. But it had been puppy love, the first flush of learning about men and women together. Maybe it would have developed into more if they'd had the time to explore it, but they hadn't. Since then, she'd kept her relationships with men easy ones, not expecting more than friendship, not *wanting* more than that.

Until Jed.

Brianne suddenly wished she could talk to her mother about all of it. Yet on the other hand, her heart was telling her not to take the safe route this time, to take a risk with Jed, hoping he'd learn to love again.

Was that why she'd decided to continue working with him even though it hurt?

When Bea saw her daughter's headlights approach the house, she quickly waved everyone into place. All the guests scurried for corners of the dining room, where the lights were out and they'd be hidden. Brianne had been positioning candles on the cake and had lit the final one when she scrambled to find a place to hide, too.

Backing up against someone, she murmured an apology.

A deep voice made her jump. "Close quarters."

Jed's voice rippled down her spine and she shivered. One of Lily's aunts, who had been putting food in the refrigerator, hurried over to the same corner and brushed against Brianne, pushing her tighter against Jed.

Brianne heard his sharp intake of breath as she felt his arousal. She couldn't step forward again because of Lily's aunt. If she made any noise, she'd alert Lily to the fact that they were all hiding.

Jed's hands were firm on Brianne's shoulders, as if he was protecting them both from further contact. Even his gentle clasp could make her tremble, and she sensed that he knew that because he loosened his fingers. She felt him take another deep breath.

It seemed like hours before Lily and Megan burst through the door. Everyone yelled "Surprise" and Brianne could finally move forward. Yet she didn't want to, and Jed didn't nudge her away. They simply stood there while everyone else hugged Lily, wishing her a happy birthday.

Amid all the noise, Jed murmured close to Brianne's ear, "I think she's surprised."

Lily was flushed and laughing, her eyes wide. Brianne could see that Megan was just as excited as her mom.

Even with Jed still so close, Brianne somehow found her voice. "I'd better go wish her a happy birthday."

Doug had his arm around Lily when Brianne approached them. Lily hugged Brianne and said, "Thanks for getting Mom to invite him."

But Brianne just shook her head. "I didn't. She invited Doug on her own. Maybe she's decided having a computer expert in the family might be a good thing."

Releasing Brianne, Lily laughed. "Wouldn't *that* be a birthday present." She spied Jed over by the buffet table but didn't have a chance to say anything else as another relative came up to hug her.

As Brianne had promised, she helped Bea make sure everyone had enough to eat and drink. Unfortunately, by the time she was ready to eat herself, the only seat in the house was a chair beside Jed's. Deciding not to put either of them through that, she went to the kitchen, set her food on the counter and then stared at it blankly, her appetite gone.

A few minutes later, Jed came into the kitchen, his expression serious. "Did you come in here to hide?"

"I'm not hiding," she said defiantly.

"You're not eating, either."

"Too much excitement, I guess."

"Excitement over a birthday party, or excitement over what happened in that corner back there?"

Jed was always honest. She just wasn't used to talking about a subject as private as a man's arousal. "I'm sorry if it was awkward—"

"It wasn't your fault, Brianne. It was just one of those things. We're attracted to each other, but we know it's best if we don't act on it."

Maybe *he* was sure about that, but she certainly wasn't. Not anymore. He was her boss, but she could always find another job. Yes, he was older, but that didn't mean they didn't want the same things in life. So what if he was more experienced? She was a fast study.

Still, she knew Jed had an iron will and even if she loved him...

Loved him.

The thought hit her like a thunderbolt. She'd known she was attracted to him, known she *could* fall in love with him. But did she actually love him?

"What's wrong?" he asked, as if he could tell something had changed her suddenly.

"Nothing. I guess I'm just a little tired. I've been running errands all day and..."

Stepping closer, he brushed an errant curl behind her ear. "If we're going to work together, we have to figure out how to do this."

"Do what?"

"Be together without turning each other inside out. I don't want to treat you like a stranger."

Until she came to grips with what she was feeling, until she decided whether it was better to stay at Beechwood Family Practice they needed to simply have a casual relationship. "Maybe we can just be friends," she suggested.

"Maybe we can." His voice was deep and husky, as if he wanted much more than friendship, too.

Megan came running into the kitchen then, calling, "Dr. Jed. Brianne. Mommy's going to open her presents. Come see.'' She'd been running so fast she barreled right into Jed's legs.

Crouching down, he caught her. ''Whoa there,'' he said with a laugh. ''Does your mommy have a lot of presents?''

''Lots and lots.'' Megan spread out her arms as if the stack were as big as a mountain.

Smiling, he straightened. ''Well, we better go watch her then. I don't think I've ever seen that many presents.''

After a grin at Brianne, Megan put her little hand in Jed's and tugged him along. ''Come on. You can sit beside me.''

The expression on Jed's face was a mixture of joy and pain. Brianne understood why now as he let Megan tug him into the living room. He sat down on the floor beside her so they'd both have a good view of everything Lily opened.

Brianne thought again about the team that did volunteer work in South America. On Monday she'd call and find out how far her application had gotten and whether or not that might be a solution to her dilemma of loving Jed.

On Monday afternoon, Brianne closed the door to her and Lily's office and took the brochure for Project Voyage out of her purse. She should have a few uninterrupted minutes to make a phone call. Jed was in a meeting with a pharmaceutical rep. Lily was picking up dry cleaning over her lunch break, and Dr. Olsen had left for the hospital.

When Brianne dialed the number on the brochure and told the receptionist she wanted to inquire about her application, she was patched through to a pleasant sounding woman named Zoie Poist.

"Can I help you?" Miss Poist asked.

"My name's Brianne Barrington. I sent an application in to Project Voyage in April. Can you tell me if it was rejected or—"

"If your application had been rejected, you would have received a letter within a few weeks. Hold on a minute and let me check the computer. We're processing a batch of them now. We've gotten a bit behind in the last few months—lack of help, that sort of thing. But the voyage team leaves at the end of May, so we have to get all these processed in the next month or so. Let me see now…Barrington…Brianne M. Your application is in Dr. Tartuff's office. That's a good sign. Hold on a minute. Maybe I can get an answer for you."

Although leaving Sawyer Springs could be difficult, it might be just what she needed right now, Brianne mused. Loving Jed would only bring her heartache if she stayed. Even if she switched positions with Lily and worked mainly with Dr. Olsen, she'd still see Jed every day.

Miss Poist was back two minutes later and there was a smile in her voice. "Your name is on the list for an interview. Dr. Tartuff was going to give you a call next week. When can you come to Minneapolis?"

Brianne would need to give a few days' notice so a temp could be hired. If she left Sunday, she could have the interview on Monday and fly back from Minneapolis Monday evening. She'd only have to miss one day of work.

"I can be there for an interview next Monday," she announced.

"Let me check Dr. Tartuff's calendar." A moment later Miss Poist said, "It looks as if he's free at eleven. Is that good for you?"

"That would be terrific."

"Do you have an e-mail address?"

After Brianne rattled off the one she used on her laptop, Miss Poist gave her the address for Project Voyage. "E-mail me once you know where you'll be staying and I'll reply with directions. We look forward to meeting you."

When Brianne hung up, she studied the brochure on her desk, remembering how excited she'd been when she'd filled out the application. It would still be exciting to work on the team. But now she saw the tour of volunteer duty as the way to escape her love for Jed.

Chapter Nine

On Monday evening when Jed brought firewood in from the shed, he was still puzzling over Brianne's absence at work that day. Dr. Olsen had merely told him she'd asked for a day of leave. Lily had been closemouthed about it, too, simply saying that Brianne had private business to take care of.

Private business that had something to do with her parents' bequest, maybe? For the past few days, he'd thought more about that directorship. Becoming involved in plastic surgery for children at a center such as Brianne had planned would be rewarding work. But was he ready to deal exclusively with children?

Crouching near the fireplace, he set down his burden of firewood. As he was stacking it in the cubicle, Al came in. "I saw the ground meat in the refrigerator. What's for supper?" he asked.

"Ground turkey tacos or ground turkey spaghetti. Take your pick."

"Spaghetti. I guess you'll have to show me how to make it so I can eat healthy after you're gone."

Al had taken to eating a healthier diet as long as Jed prepared it.

When his dad lowered himself into the recliner and stretched out his leg, Jed decided this was as good a time as any to broach the conversation he wanted to have with him.

After he stacked the last of the logs, he asked his dad, "Have you ever considered selling this place?"

Al's eyes widened. "Where would I go?" he asked gruffly. "You want to put me in a nursing home?"

It was probably his father's worst fear and one that could become a reality if Jed didn't stay in Sawyer Springs. "No, that's not what I had in mind. A place with fewer steps and good insulation might be something to think about. In fact, you and I could find a place. I could buy a two-story and make the top floor mine and the bottom floor yours. We could share a kitchen if you want, or we could remodel and each have our own."

"You're going to stay here then?" Al sounded astonished.

"It feels right to be back. I don't see the town the same way as I used to."

His father looked totally taken aback. "I wouldn't let you buy the house, you know. I could use what I get from this place for my half."

"Or…you could let me make the investment, and you could use the proceeds from the sale of this house for the nest egg you might need."

Al ruminated for a few seconds, then looked his son in the eye. "Are you sure this is what you want to do? I don't want you staying here out of some sense of noble sacrifice.''

''It wouldn't be a sacrifice. I need to put my life back together again, and I think this would be a way to start.''

''Sure you don't want to start housekeeping with Brianne instead?''

''That's never going to happen. Brianne deserves more than I can give her.'' Jed decided to test the waters in another area, and changed the subject. ''I talked to Chris and Ellie last week. They're thinking of flying in this weekend. How do you feel about that?''

''Both of them coming in...with you here, too?''

''That's what we're thinking. Can you handle all that commotion?''

Al looked away from his son and his voice was thick as he answered, ''I think I can handle it just fine.''

His father might be a crotchety old coot some of the time, but like most dads, he basically wanted to be close to his kids. Jed realized he hadn't taken enough care with the bonds in his life and he wasn't about to let this one disintegrate. Tomorrow morning he'd call a real estate agent and find out what was on the market.

On Wednesday evening the Sawyer Springs Food Bank bustled with activity. It was the end of February and the spring clothing drive always brought people from every walk of life to assist. Lily and Megan were helping to sort children's clothes. Brianne stood at the drop-off counter, passing boxes in the right direction for volunteers to pack. She kept thinking about her interview in Minneapolis at the beginning of the week and what she was going to do if Project Voyage accepted her for the team. She had liked Dr. Tartuff and everyone she'd met there. But leaving Sawyer Springs would be wrenching.

And leaving Jed…

Trying to keep her mind on the task in front of her, she heard the bell over the door ring several times. She accepted clothes mechanically, handing them on until she finally raised her head and saw…Jed.

"I didn't know you'd be helping here tonight." His tone was casual but the nerve in his jaw was working.

They'd hardly said two words to each other since she'd returned from Minneapolis, except for whatever conversation was necessary about their patients. "Lily and I signed up."

He probably wouldn't have stopped by this evening if he'd known she would be here, Brianne realized. Working side by side this week had been difficult for her. Since she'd realized she loved him, ignoring everything that had passed between them and trying to deny the effect of inadvertent touches seemed impossible. She'd noticed the flashes of emotion in Jed's eyes, too, and known he was as affected as she was. But he'd apparently set a course for himself, and there was nothing she could do about that. She loved him, but he was obviously closed to that emotion because it could cause him pain again. She'd felt that way, too, until she'd met him. Then, her heart had decided he was worth the risk.

The box of clothes he set on her counter was full. "Dad decided to clean out his closet. There are suits in here he said he'll never wear again. They're out of style, but I thought somebody might be able to use them.''

To avoid his gaze, she examined the contents of the box and saw two sweaters along with the suits. ''These are in beautiful condition.''

''They're my contribution. Or did you only want summer things?''

''Oh, no. Anything's fine.''

As Brianne began to put the clothes back into the box, Jed helped her. Somehow their hands tangled and their gazes met. As always, her pulse quickened and she ached for what they could have together.

Pulling away from her, he stuffed his hands into his jeans pockets. ''Ellie and Chris are arriving tomorrow night. I didn't want to take the time to do this while they're here.''

''I understand. Does your dad know they're coming?''

Jed almost smiled. ''I thought I'd better tell him so he didn't have a heart attack when they arrived. He seems excited. As excited as he gets. I have orders to stop at the grocery store and stock up on everything we might need.''

''It sounds as if you're excited, too.''

''It will be good to see them.''

Just then, the bell over the door sounded again and a man called Jed's name.

Jed glanced over his shoulder. A smile turned up his lips as he greeted the mayor of Sawyer Springs. Lou Devors was in his mid-forties, a genial man who kept an eagle-eye on the Sawyer Springs budget. The residents of Sawyer Springs had elected him for a third term, which showed their support for the efficient way he ran the town.

Lou shook Jed's hand. "Your father told me I could find you here. Sorry to barge in on your private time, but I didn't want to bother you at the office."

"I don't mind." After Jed introduced Lou, he explained to Brianne, "Lou and I used to play one-on-one basketball on weekends. He was a few years ahead of me in school but he kept me out of trouble."

"He didn't have time for trouble," Lou said with a wave of his hand. "You were hell-bent on making tracks out of here. I was surprised to hear you'd come back and accepted a job at Beechwood. If you're going to be around for a while, at least until the end of the year, I want to invite you to fill one of our city council seats. Joe Briggs and his family moved, so one's vacant. Since your forefathers founded Sawyer Springs, it only seemed fitting I ask you. You can run for the seat yourself next term if you have a mind to."

"It's an honor to be asked."

"When I suggested your name, there was a consensus. No in-fighting for once. What do you say?"

Brianne held her breath as she waited. Would Jed be leaving or staying?

"Meetings are once a month?" Jed asked.

Lou nodded. "A special one every now and then. But that doesn't happen too often."

"It sounds like something I'd like to do."

"Are you going to be around on Saturday?"

"I should be. I'm not on-call this weekend."

"Stop in at the office. I'm there Saturday mornings. We'll talk about it and sign the official papers." After he shook Jed's hand and nodded to Brianne, the mayor exited with the same quick step with which he'd come in.

"You're going to stay in Sawyer Springs?" Brianne asked Jed.

"Yes."

She knew she should ask the next question, but was almost afraid of the answer about the directorship of the plastic surgery center. Had he made a decision about that, too?

His gaze dropped to the box of clothes, then to Brianne's hands, as if remembering the chemistry when their fingers had touched. As if remembering everything that had happened between them up until now... Then he asked, "Will *you* be around this weekend?"

"I should be."

"I'll give you my decision about the directorship on Saturday. I know you want to get this project started." He lifted the box of clothes. "Where would you like me to put these?"

Motioning to a corner where volunteers were stacking the men's things, she watched as Jed easily carried the heavy box. He was wearing jeans, a flannel shirt and his insulated vest. He'd never looked more like an outdoors man. She loved everything about him, and knew that if he accepted the directorship, he would be opening himself to life again, and maybe could open his heart to love.

Hope lifted *her* heart when he stopped at the counter again. There seemed to be a volume of unsaid words between them. Finally, he broke the silence. "I'll see you in the morning."

Her hands trembled as she held on to the counter, allowing her dreams to come alive once more.

On Friday afternoon, Brianne received a call from Project Voyage. She learned she was accepted on the team if she wanted the position, but Dr. Tartuff would need her answer in two weeks. Although she was happy about the offer, when she thought about leaving Jed and Sawyer Springs, she was bombarded with a terrible sadness. Jed's answer tomorrow about the directorship would give her direction, maybe give her a glimpse of what he was feeling about her.

That evening Brianne was helping Lily clean up the supper dishes when the telephone rang. She was closest to the phone so she picked it up. "Hello?"

"Brianne, is that you?"

It was Al's gruff voice, and she smiled. "Yes, Al, it's me."

"Well, good. I was hoping you would be there tonight. What are you doing for the next couple of hours?"

Warily, Brianne answered, "I'm not sure."

"I've got all my kids here and we'd like you to meet Chris and Ellie. Why don't you come over for some beer and chips?"

He'd used the pronoun "we." "Jed wants me to come over?"

"We want you to meet our family. Come on, what do you say?"

She was surprised and touched by Al's invitation. She would love to meet Jed's brother and sister. Did that mean he was thinking about letting her into his life?

"As soon as I freshen up, I'll be there."

When she hung up the phone, she was smiling and felt happier than she had all week.

It took her only a few minutes to run a brush through her hair and add a light coat of lipstick. She dressed in a sea-green sweater and skirt with shoes instead of boots. They'd had a couple of warmer days this week and most of the icy spots on sidewalks were gone, at least until tomorrow, when the weatherman was calling for snow again.

After bidding Lily and Megan good-night, she drove to Jed's, excited and lighthearted. She wondered if Chris would resemble Jed, if Ellie was petite or tall like her brother.

After Brianne rang the bell, she waited expectantly.

The door opened and Jed stood there, a look of surprise on his face. "Brianne."

Al was beside him in an instant. "I invited her over to join the party. I thought she'd like to meet Ellie and Chris. Isn't that a great idea?"

Something deep and intense flashed in Jed's eyes. Then he nodded. "I'm sure Ellie and Chris would love to meet Brianne. Come on in."

Brianne suddenly felt like a fool. If this was Al's attempt at matchmaking, it was going to fall flat. She would never have put Jed on the spot like this, and she hoped he knew it.

Once she was inside, she didn't have the opportunity to speak to him alone because she got caught up in the introductions. Chris did indeed resemble Jed, taking after their father. Chris's hair was brown instead of black. Glancing at the picture of the Sawyer family, Brianne decided Ellie looked like her mother.

Both Chris and Ellie were warm and friendly, and Brianne soon felt her awkwardness slip away. Ray smiled at her while Jed introduced her to three more of Al's friends.

After Jed had taken Brianne's coat, Ellie put her

arm through the crook of Brianne's elbow and guided her to the sofa. "Come talk to me."

Lowering her voice, she murmured, "Dad said you and Jed were seeing each other, but you don't want to go too public with it because you work together at Beechwood."

"We're not exactly 'seeing' each other," Brianne said. She didn't confide in strangers easily, and even though Ellie was friendly and interested, Brianne wasn't about to discuss her feelings for Jed.

"Are you saying Dad misled me?"

Apparently Ellie was as bluntly honest as her brother. "Jed and I have seen each other outside of work now and then."

Ellie's gaze went to Jed, who had grabbed a beer and then returned to the living room. His eyes were on Brianne and she quickly looked away.

Ellie smiled. "Hmm. Well, there's something in the air. Dad's probably trying to promote it. You know about Caroline?"

"I know she was Jed's wife."

"Dad didn't like her at all. Can't say I blame him. She didn't like a thing about Sawyer Springs or Dad's blue-collar background."

Brianne didn't feel comfortable discussing all of this with Jed's sister, but she didn't know how to break away without appearing unfriendly.

Suddenly, though, as if Jed had guessed Ellie had cornered Brianne, he was at her side. "Why don't you come to the kitchen with me? You can get something to drink and a few snacks."

She wasn't the least bit hungry or thirsty but she'd follow Jed anywhere.

That idea gave her pause.

Once in the kitchen, Jed motioned to the cooler of beer and then waved to the counter. "Or there's wine. Ellie brought that because she doesn't share our taste in beer."

"Beer's fine," Brianne said absently, distracted by the masculine shadow of beard on Jed's jaw, the mesmerizing heat in his eyes. When she stooped to the cooler, he did the same, and they found themselves nose to nose.

Pulling a bottle from the ice, Jed straightened and handed it to her. "Was Ellie giving you the third degree?"

"Not exactly. Jed, I want you to know I only came tonight because I thought the invitation was from you, too. Your dad made it sound like that."

"He's so damn happy to have us all here again he wants to tell everybody about it. Last night after Chris and Ellie arrived, he called his poker club to come over. Chris and Ellie were exhausted, but Dad kept them up talking until past two o'clock." Jed picked up a plate of cookies and held it toward Brianne. "From the bakery."

When she took one, their gazes met again, and she wanted to hear his decision so badly, she thought she'd explode.

Loud voices floated in from the living room, and Ellie called, "Brianne, Jed. Come in here. I want to take pictures so we can update the photo album."

Jed groaned. "Always the camera buff. You'd think she'd stop producing and directing when she's not working."

Brianne laughed. "It's not easy to leave your work at home when you love it."

After a pause, Jed agreed. "I guess that's true. Come on. Let's get this over with."

But it wasn't that easy. Ellie knew what kind of pictures she wanted and wasn't satisfied with just any pose. After she snapped Al with his friends, she gave the camera to Ray and he took one of the Sawyer family.

With enthusiasm, she took the camera back again and motioned to Jed and Brianne. "Over there, by the fireplace. Put your arm around her, Jed."

"You don't have to," Brianne murmured.

His arm went around her as if it belonged there. "I always try to give Ellie what she wants. It saves a hassle."

Brianne remembered all the other times she'd felt Jed's arms around her. His embrace always excited her, yet in an odd way, made her feel safe, too. She could feel his heat through his shirtsleeve and she wondered if he could feel hers. When she dared to glance up at him, she knew he could. They couldn't deny the chemistry between them even if everything else was in a muddle.

"Have you ever seen these old photo albums?" Ellie asked Brianne, pointing to a stack on the coffee table after the picture-taking was finished.

When Brianne shook her head, Jed released her. She found it hard to move away from him but she knew she had to.

Then she went to sit beside Ellie again.

"After Mom died, we didn't take many pictures," Ellie admitted sadly. "It wasn't until I was a teenager I picked up a camera again. Then I shot mostly scenery and animals, not family. Come see what Jed looked like as a kid."

"Oh, Ellie," he protested.

Beside Ellie, Brianne eagerly studied the small boy with a lock of hair falling into his eyes.

"Jed must have been around six in that picture," Ellie explained.

He was standing beside a wagon.

Al peered over Ellie's shoulder. "That's the wagon I told you about. On one of Trisha's visits, I lugged her around in that thing—"

Al stopped abruptly and there was sudden silence, as if a taboo subject had been broached. Everyone's gaze was on Jed.

His voice was strained as he said, "Believe it or not, I have a picture of that. But it's in storage in L.A. along with all the other stuff I didn't need in Alaska." Then, clearing his throat, he turned to glance at the fireplace. "Hey, Chris. Throw another log on the fire, would you?"

Brianne so wanted to go to Jed and take his hand and tell him she understood the force of a memory. But he began a conversation with Ray then, and she knew he was still pushing down all of his feelings about Trisha and everything that had happened. That one night he'd shared with her, too much had risen to the surface. Brianne just hoped that had been the beginning of a healing process.

She didn't have the chance to spend another minute alone with Jed. There were too many people, too many conversations. It was ten when she finally looked at her watch. Not wanting to wear out her welcome, she went to the kitchen for her coat.

As she was taking it from the back of a chair, Al joined her. "I'm glad you could come."

He was a kind, well-meaning man and she didn't

want to take him to task for getting her there under false pretenses. "I'm glad I came, too."

When Al helped her with her coat, he said in a low voice, "Don't you give up on my boy. He just needs a push in the right direction."

As Brianne buttoned her coat, she argued, "Pushing too hard could send him in the other direction."

But Al obviously didn't agree. He gave her arm a squeeze and advised, "Be patient."

After Brianne returned to the living room to say goodbye to everyone, Jed came over and walked her to the door.

"I'll see you tomorrow," he reminded her. "I don't know when. After I stop in at the mayor's office, I'll make rounds at the hospital. It will be after that."

"Anytime's fine."

Reaching out, he straightened the lapel of her coat. "I'm glad Dad asked you to come over tonight. Ellie and Chris enjoyed meeting you."

He was looking down at her as if he wanted to take her into his arms and kiss her. She wanted that again. She'd dreamed of it. She'd hoped for it.

But then Jed withdrew and took a step away.

As Brianne started the car, she knew she and Jed would never have a chance together unless he stopped backing away.

The pizza delivery man was leaving Lily's Victorian as Jed ascended the porch steps. Brianne was still at the door, and when she saw him, her smile was strained. He knew she was eager for his decision. He should have given it to her last night.

Last night had confirmed what he'd known all

along. He wasn't ready for the family gatherings and the kids and the commitment that an involvement with someone brought. He was better off single, looking out for his dad, starting a new venture that would set his life on the course he wanted it to go.

She opened the storm door. "We're having an early supper. We've got plenty. Want to join us?"

As soon as Jed stepped inside, he knew he couldn't talk to Brianne while Megan and Lily were within earshot.

Lily must have sensed that because she called from the kitchen, "Join us, Jed. Then you and Brianne can have a private discussion. Doug bought a big-screen TV. Megan and I are going to pick out a video and take it over to his place to watch."

Jed didn't want to prolong this for anyone, but joining them for supper, then talking to Brianne when the others left, would be best.

As soon as they all sat down at the table and started on slices of pizza, bright-eyed Megan grinned at him. "We're going skating tomorrow."

With a string of cheese dripping down her chin, she looked so precious, Jed felt as if his heart were cracking. He could imagine Trisha with pizza sauce on her lips, sticky cheese on her fingers. "We're supposed to get a dusting of snow tonight. You'll have to wear your hat and mittens," he answered.

Megan nodded solemnly. "And take hot chocolate."

Jed had to laugh. "That's definitely a necessity."

"It's not a skating outing without hot chocolate," Lily added, trying to keep the conversation going, since Brianne was so quiet.

Finally, Brianne asked, "When are Chris and Ellie leaving?"

"Tomorrow morning. Dad's going to miss them. The house will seem quiet again."

"Maybe it won't be so long until you all get together next time."

That was a promise Chris and Ellie had made—that it wouldn't be so long between visits. Jed had told them his plans to buy a house where their dad could get around more easily, and they had encouraged it. They'd decided they wouldn't let life become so busy that they wouldn't see each other for four years ever again. Jed hoped that was a promise they could all keep.

It seemed to take forever, but finally Megan finished her pizza. Lily cleaned off the table while Brianne loaded the dishwasher. Afterward, Megan ran to get her coat and returned with it and Penelope, too. As Lily zipped Megan's parka for her, Megan tucked the doll protectively under her arm and grinned up at Brianne. "Penelope's going to watch the big TV, too."

"You tell her to remember everything she sees so she can tell me all about it."

With a nod, Megan gave Brianne a huge hug. The picture made Jed's gut twist. That doll meant everything to Megan because it had come from Brianne.

After Lily and Megan left through the kitchen door, Jed motioned to the living room. "Why don't we sit in there?"

Once they were seated on the sofa, he began, "I'm honored that you considered me to be the director of this project. I know it's important to you."

"But?"

"But I don't think it's for me. In fact…I'm going to open a private practice."

Brianne's eyes were wide with astonishment. "You're going to leave Beechwood?"

"Don't you think that's best? Although we work together well, it's just too difficult to be around you, Brianne. I'm always thinking about kissing you instead of focusing my mind where it's supposed to be. As a doctor, I can't be distracted."

"You don't have to set up a private practice. I can—"

"It's not just you. Dr. Olsen intends to bring in two more doctors. I want to work on my own for several reasons. The main one is that in a private practice, I can devote one day a week at least to patients who don't have insurance coverage. I can make a difference in Sawyer Springs. Maybe that way I can get a free clinic started and have other doctors volunteer."

"That's a wonderful idea." She was looking up at him with admiration and respect, something he'd never seen in Caroline's eyes. But there was sadness there, too.

Brianne lowered her gaze to her lap. "Jed, I'm going to leave Beechwood, too."

"What?"

"I've been offered a position on a team for Project Voyage. They're sailing for South America in May and I'm going to be on the ship."

His gut clenched. "What about the plastic surgery center?"

"I've already called a few people I'd like to see on the board and they've said yes. All that's left is the paperwork. I can have the foundation set up before I leave. Maybe you can give me names of doctors in the plastic surgery field you feel would be good candidates for the directorship.''

Her news stunned him. Although he'd planned to turn down the directorship and leave Beechwood, he was staying in Sawyer Springs. The thought of Brianne not being here...

''Are you sure you want to leave Sawyer Springs?''

Her gaze held his. ''Remember when you told me I wasn't old enough to understand turning points? You were wrong about that. I've had a couple of them and this is just one more. My feelings for you...'' She stopped.

He felt so many things for her, too. The idea that he wouldn't see her again for months...

Reaching out, he slid his hand into her silky hair. Though he told himself he shouldn't, he couldn't keep from running his thumb along her delicate jawline. He couldn't stop himself from leaning forward, wanting a last kiss.

She must have wanted that, too, because as he bent his head, she leaned closer. Then she was in his arms and he was kissing her.

He didn't want to think about endings. He didn't want to think about why he couldn't let go of the past and let Brianne into his life. All he knew was that she was soft and sweet and willing. She'd brought joy and life and sparkle back to him again, and he didn't want to give that up.

With a groan, he pushed his tongue into her mouth and she responded with a fervor he knew was part of her, with a passion that went deep despite her innocence. A few moments later, he was caressing her breasts and she was making soft erotic sounds, asking for more. Mindlessly, Jed lifted Brianne's sweater over her head and unhooked her bra. She unfastened the buttons on his shirt. When her hands pressed against his chest, he sucked in a very deep breath.

"Oh, Jed," Brianne murmured. "I love you."

Everything inside of him stilled. Nobility fought against basic need and he made himself stop touching her, stop kissing her, stop longing for the physical satisfaction she could give him. He shook his head. "I can't do this. It's wrong."

"It's wrong because I love you?"

"Yes, Brianne. I don't want you to love me. I can't return it. I won't take advantage of you."

"You're not taking advantage of me. I know full well what I'm doing."

"And if you get pregnant?"

"Then I'd have your child to love, too."

Nothing she could have said would have affected him more. His throat tightened and his lungs didn't seem to want to fill with air. The pain he felt was greater than anything he'd ever experienced.

"That just proves how young you are, Brianne. Children need two parents who want to be together."

He didn't think he'd ever seen Brianne really angry before. Now her cheeks flushed red as she righted her clothes. Her beautiful aquamarine eyes shot furious sparks at him. "Young? I'm not young because I have dreams. I know what it would be like to take care of a child alone. I've seen how Lily struggles. But it would be worth it to have your child. The problem is you can't let yourself be a dad again. You can't let yourself be happy."

"Brianne—"

"Do you know what you're doing? You're taking the safe route again. I know I can't begin to understand what it's like to lose a child. I can only imagine it. I understand that after Trisha drowned, you needed safety. You escaped to Alaska, where basic needs were all that mattered. That was safe."

"You've no right to judge my choices," he growled, angry now, too, because she'd hit too many nails on the head.

"I know I have no rights where you're concerned, because that's the way you want it. You found your way back to your dad, but now you think that's enough. It's not enough, Jed. The human heart is made to love…to be filled with love. I know love hurts. Goodness knows, that's why I've been fighting everything I feel for you. But unfortunately, love takes over sometimes and we don't have any control over that." She shook her head hopelessly. "You won't let your heart control you. You won't give love a chance."

After Jed buttoned his shirt, he stood and tucked it into his jeans. "I don't think we have any more to say. I'll put out feelers to help Dr. Olsen find a replacement for me. The sooner I leave, the better. In the meantime, we'll just have to keep our personal feelings away from our work."

"That's the difference between you and me, Jed. Apparently you can separate yourself from your feelings altogether. I can't. Don't worry about leaving quickly. I'll hand in my resignation on Monday. It will be easier for Dr. Olsen to find a replacement for me rather than you. I'll work on getting the plastic surgery foundation set up."

He thought about not seeing Brianne again, not

working with her, not feeling her warmth. But after what had just happened, he knew neither of them had a choice.

Silently he picked up his coat, put it on and walked away from the Victorian, leaving a piece of himself behind.

Chapter Ten

By the time Sunday afternoon rolled around, Jed needed some type of activity to distract his thoughts. After he'd left Brianne yesterday, he'd told himself over and over again that he'd done the right thing for both of them. Although he'd spent the evening with Ellie, Chris and his dad, Ellie had noted that he was quieter than usual. He'd explained his silence by chalking it up to a long week. That explanation had seemed to satisfy his brother and his father, but Ellie had given him one of her knowing looks.

Since he'd given Chris his bed and was sleeping on the sofa downstairs, Jed remembered every detail of the night he and Brianne had spent during the snowstorm in front of the fire. This morning, before Ellie had left with Chris for the airport, she'd taken Jed aside and told him that the next time she talked to him, she might be engaged. She'd been dating a real estate broker for the past few months, and she thought this time she might have found the right man.

With his goodbye hug, Jed wished her much happiness. She'd looked deep into his eyes and wished him the same.

He'd felt happiness again with Brianne in his life. He'd been shocked by her news that she was going to leave Sawyer Springs. Yet she was young and adventurous and had her whole life ahead of her. Why shouldn't she go wherever she wanted to go…do whatever she wanted to do?

Still, when he thought about her leaving, he was filled with an aching longing that wouldn't go away. After she resigned on Monday, he might never see her again.

With Chris and Ellie gone now, Al was dozing in his favorite chair. Jed told his dad he was going out for a while, and grabbed his coat. He had to see Brianne again. She was going skating this afternoon with Megan and Lily. She didn't even have to know he was there. He could just get a last glimpse of her.

There had been a dusting of snow last night, but the sun was shining brightly and had already melted the spots that weren't shaded. As he parked in the lot near the lake, he saw part of the surface sparkling like diamonds. The area where many skaters were gathered was still coated with white powder. Already there were the makings of a bonfire. On the table set up along the edge of the lake were big thermoses of hot chocolate.

Stopping by the table, he looked over the crowd until he spied Lily and Megan skating. As he canvassed the area, he finally saw Brianne seated on the bench away from everyone else. He knew that yellow cap of hers just as he knew Megan's pink one. The band of yellow on her ski jacket seemed golden in the sunlight. It wasn't like her to sit on the sidelines, but he knew she had a lot on her mind, just as he had a lot on his.

Even though it was early March, there wasn't any wind. The branches on the pines and cedars surrounding the lake were still. Beech and aspen reached up into the blue sky, and Jed thought about spring coming and the promise of new life.

New life in Sawyer Springs without Brianne Barrington.

Children called to each other and to their parents. Two boys raced across the ice in an imitation of a speed skating event. Out of the corner of his eye, Jed saw it all, although he still focused on Brianne.

Catching sight of Megan and Lily again, he didn't know why he felt uneasy when Megan glided toward a copse of cedars. Then he remembered playing football with Rob, and the ice fisherman who had used an ax. What if the fisherman had returned to the same spot recently? With the warmer weather, the dusting of snow last night…

Although he'd intended to stay on the edge of the crowd, Jed found himself running toward Megan, shouting to warn her away from that spot. But Megan didn't seem to hear him. He shouted again and had almost reached Lily when the unthinkable happened. He heard a crack and then a splash. Megan disappeared.

Lily gave an anguished cry.

A woman who had been skating close to Megan gasped in horror and backed away from the cracking ice.

His heart thudding, his blood racing, Jed plucked

his cell phone from his belt, tossed it to the woman and yelled, "Call 911. Now!"

He could feel Lily at his side and hear her sob of terror. He commanded, "Stay back or you'll fall in, too. I'll get her."

Seconds were ticking by. The lake was shallow where Megan had fallen in, and he could see her pink jacket. Jed dropped down onto his stomach, slowly slid forward to the edge of the hole and reached for her sleeve. But the cold, wet material slipped through his fingers.

Fear clutched him as he stretched his arm toward her again, determined to save her without losing more precious moments. This time his fingers clenched the fabric and he tugged her to him, carefully drawing her onto solid ice.

In an instant, Lily and Brianne were by his side. Lily was sobbing and seemed to be in shock as she stared at her still daughter.

As Jed checked Megan's pulse and breathing, Brianne said in a tense murmur, "Her chest isn't rising and falling."

There was an irregular pulse but no respiration. She could have struck her head...she could have...

Jed tilted Megan's head back to open the airway. Brianne was already taking off her jacket to cover the little girl. "Do you have a pulse?" she asked.

There was a moan from Lily, and Jed knew she had stopped being a nurse and was suffering as a mother.

"It's irregular. She's not breathing." Pinching Megan's nose, he dipped his head and began mouth-to-mouth resuscitation.

Responding, Megan coughed, regurgitated and began breathing on her own. But her eyes didn't flutter open, and Jed didn't like her still-weak pulse and her blue-tinged skin.

Tears ran down Lily's cheeks as she held her daughter's arm.

Jed knew they shouldn't move Megan. Because of hypothermia, they had to get the wet clothes off of her, but they needed a sheltered place to do it. As Jed monitored the five-year-old, someone brought blankets. By the time Brianne covered Megan with those, too, the paramedics had arrived. They started an IV, then rushed her to the ambulance, where they removed her wet clothes and wrapped her in blankets while the ambulance heater ran full throttle.

Jed barely noticed his wet jeans, the snow falling from his jacket as he climbed into the ambulance with Megan.

His gaze locked with Brianne's before the attendant closed the door. He saw the anguish there and felt her plea for him to do everything he could to help this little girl she dearly loved.

At Sawyer Springs General, Megan was rushed into the emergency room. Jed made sure the pulmonary specialist was called in, as well as a neurologist. He wanted the best team gathered for Megan's care. She still wasn't awake and that troubled him. He was determined to stay with her, to do absolutely everything he could to make sure she lived.

He would not lose Megan as he'd lost Trisha.

Three hours later, Brianne waited outside Megan's ICU room. The five-year-old had been placed on a cardiac monitor and an electronic blood pressure machine. An IV was running with warm saline, and a warming blanket covered her. Although she was breathing on her own, she was still unconscious, and Brianne could see the worry on everyone's faces— the doctors who went in and out, Lily's, Jed's. Jed hadn't spoken to her since she'd worked with him at the lake, but the lines on his face were deep and the worry in his eyes obvious. She knew this was taking him back somewhere he didn't want to be.

He'd changed into a pair of scrubs and now came out of Megan's room. Lily was sitting by her daughter's bed holding her hand. Brianne knew there wasn't anything she could say or do to make this easier for Lily...or for Jed. He had risked his life to save Megan. He could have fallen through that ice as easily as she had! Only his quick thinking and decisive actions had saved her.

"What can we do?" Brianne asked him now, hoping he had something in mind.

He shook his head and there was raw pain in his eyes. "Her CT scans look okay, as does everything else. If she doesn't come around soon..."

He turned away from Brianne and glanced through the glass window.

"What are you afraid of?"

"I'm afraid I didn't pull her out in time, and oxygen deprivation is the problem."

"You did everything you could."

He gave a humorless laugh. "Yeah. Well, it might not have been enough."

As they both stared through the window, Brianne said, "I understand how hard this must be for you. But you did save her."

"Not if she doesn't wake up. I'll have failed again."

If Megan died, Brianne knew this loss would devastate Jed as much as the first. He might never return to the land of loving and happiness. There had to be something she could do...something they could all do.

In spite of the circumstances, there seemed to be a wall between her and Jed. Her declaration of love had pushed them even further apart, and she knew he was thinking what good was love when this little girl was lying here unconscious. But because Brianne's parents had taught her well, because they'd loved each other above their careers during the ups and downs of married life, as well as throughout her insecurities about her feelings concerning them, she knew there was healing power in hope and love and everything they'd taught her to believe in. Megan needed love around her now.

As Doug, Bea and her husband, Charlie, came into the ICU waiting area, looking to Jed for answers, Brianne slipped away and went to the parking garage to her car. She had driven Lily and Megan to the lake, and then here after Jed had climbed into the ambulance. There was something in the car that belonged to Megan, and Brianne didn't know if it would do any good or not, but she was going to fetch Penelope and snuggle her into Megan's arms.

A few minutes later, she returned with the rag doll that had meant so much to her and now meant so much to Megan. Tears were running down Bea's cheeks as Jed spoke softly to her and her husband.

Brianne opened the glass door and stepped into Megan's cubicle. She felt Jed's gaze on her from beyond the window and knew he was wondering what she was doing.

After a squeeze to Lily's shoulder, Brianne stooped low over Megan. "I have Penelope here, honey. She's lonely without you and so are we. She needs you to take care of her. I'm going to snuggle her under this blanket with you. It would be great if you would open your eyes and talk to her and talk to us."

"Do you really think she can hear you?" Lily asked. "I know we're supposed to know these things, but we don't. I'm wondering if talking will do any good."

"She knows the sound of your voice. She knew the sound of your voice when she was in your womb. You have to believe that she can hear you. I do." Brianne was certain in her soul about that. She remembered those last days with Bobby....

When she straightened, she knew Jed had slipped into the room and was standing at the foot of the bed. "I'm not sure both of you should be in here," he whispered. "The neurologist said—"

"She needs our love, Jed. She needs all of us." Brianne opened the glass door once more and motioned to Bea, Charlie and Doug. She saw the protest start to form on Jed's lips, but she wouldn't let any amount of protest make a difference—not right now. She might be younger than he was, she might be more naive, but she believed in the power of loving, and they had to use that power to help Megan.

"We all love her," Brianne said, addressing them. "We have to believe our love can make a difference."

After she took hold of Megan's hand, she reached out and took Jed's. He looked at her as if he had no idea what she was going to do, what *they* were going to do. Yet Bea and Lily caught on quickly, and Charlie nodded, along with Doug. Holding her daughter's other hand, Lily linked her fingers with Doug's. Doug hesitantly reached for Charlie, and Charlie in turn grasped his wife's hand. Bea clasped Jed's.

"If we tell her how much we love her," Brianne said in a low voice, "and if we pray, maybe it will make a difference."

She saw Jed's eyes close. The expression on his face told her he thought it was hopeless. Yet nothing was hopeless. In fact, if she was courageous enough and stayed in Sawyer Springs...

That was a thought for another time and place.

Jed felt the warm, tight grip of Brianne's hand. He heard her murmur, "I believe in the power of love." Opening his eyes, he glanced at her and found her gaze upon him.

He didn't know if he could believe with her. He didn't know if all the love in the world could help Megan. Deep down inside, though, he knew if he didn't try to help Megan in this way, too, he'd regret it for the rest of his life.

Giving Brianne's hand a squeeze, feeling Bea's hand holding his, he closed his eyes again and tried to feel the connection. Not only did he try to feel it, he tried to add to it. Whatever compassion and caring and hope he had locked away in his heart, he offered to Megan now. He didn't know if he knew what praying was anymore, but he felt a stirring deep within that seemed to be an answer to his offering of everything good inside him. He thought he'd feel empty as he opened his heart, but he didn't. He felt full...with more to give.

When one of the monitors beeped faster, Jed

opened his eyes. Had Megan's muscles flexed? Had she—

Suddenly the little girl's eyelids fluttered. She looked down at her doll and at everybody standing around her. Then she reached out her arms to Lily. "Mommy."

Bedlam erupted. Jed said to Brianne, "Quick, get Dr. Gibson." And he went to Megan's side, keeping track of the readings on all the monitors.

A few moments later, the neurologist was in the room shooing everyone out, including Lily.

After a thorough examination of the young patient, Dr. Gibson came out of the cubicle with a wide smile. To Lily, he said, "I want to keep her here another twenty-four hours and watch her carefully. But I don't see any reason why she shouldn't make a full recovery."

Lily hugged Brianne tightly and then everyone else in the room, too, including Jed. After she released him, she hurried to her daughter's side once more.

Jed's gaze met Brianne's, and what he saw there overwhelmed him. She had told him she loved him, but he'd denied that love.

How stupid could he have been?

Even after everything Brianne had been through, she had a powerful faith. She was a remarkable young woman. Suddenly he knew that all these weeks he'd been fighting the wrong battle. Instead of battling to keep his heart closed, he should have been forcing it open.

Trisha's death had brought him grief and loss and pain and guilt. He'd become so comfortable with all of that that he'd held on to it, afraid to let go. It was his reaction to Trisha's death that had kept him in limbo for so long.

Today he had saved a little girl. Was that part of the Master's plan? He didn't know. He did know that saving Megan had saved him.

He could no longer deny that he felt so much more for Brianne than desire. He loved her.

The love in *her* gaze today had convinced him that he might have love to give. Once he'd opened his heart, he'd felt a rush of joy and happiness he hadn't felt in years. Brianne Barrington had taught him how to truly love again. He wanted her by his side every day. He wanted to see her pretty smile at the breakfast table, work beside her, sleep beside her and make love to her every night.

He had to tell her that right now.

"I need to talk to you," he insisted, his voice deep and husky. Taking her hand, he pulled her down a corridor.

"Jed, where are we going?"

He didn't take time to answer, but turned the knob on the door that led to the supply closet and pulled her inside. Switching on the light, he gazed down at her, hoping what he had to say wasn't too late.

"Don't take the job with Project Voyage," he blurted out, trying to put some of his thoughts into order.

Brianne went perfectly still. "Why shouldn't I take the job?"

This was it, and he had to get it right. "When I went to Alaska, I was a broken man. The work, the people and the life in Deep River helped put me back together again. But I didn't realize part of me was still broken. When I returned to Sawyer Springs, I didn't know what I wanted. After I met you, everything started to become clearer. Although I might be the older one..." he smiled wryly "...you've taught me so many things. I've put up every defense in the book, but somehow you managed to slip by all of them and rattle the cage I built around myself. You've shown me how love can heal. Yesterday when you told me you loved me, I should have gotten down on my knees and thanked you for it. Instead, I denied it. I thought I could be indifferent to it."

Reaching out, he cupped her cheek with his palm. "I can't deny what's between us any longer. I love you, Brianne Barrington. I want you to be my wife. If you think we haven't known each other long enough, if you need time to think about this..."

The radiance on her face stopped him. She came closer, circling his neck with her arms.

He embraced her as he'd wanted to embrace her for weeks. He was about to kiss her when she declared, "I love you, Jed Sawyer. Yes, I'll marry you."

As his lips met hers, his desire for her seemed to magnify tenfold, his love a hundredfold. He not only wanted Brianne, he needed her. All of that need drove his kiss as his tongue swept her mouth, and she responded with a passion and fervor that told him she felt the same. The kiss went on and on until he broke it and tilted his forehead against hers.

After their hearts had slowed a bit, Brianne said, "You're a hero. Do you have any idea how scared I was when you stretched out on that ice to save Megan?"

"I did what I had to do, just as you did in that room a few minutes ago."

"I didn't risk my life."

"No, you risked your love." Holding her close, he whispered, "And that's even more courageous."

Then they were kissing again, promising each other their future and everlasting love.

Epilogue

Her hand in Jed's, Brianne ran beside him under a shower of rose petals as friends and family called out good wishes. His SUV was parked at the curb, decorated with white streamers and a Just Married sign in the rear window. The door to the vehicle was open, and he scooped her up and lifted her inside. The straight skirt of her white suit didn't allow much room for climbing, and Jed obviously had seen that. He seemed to know her wants and needs before she even asked.

When he gave her a long sweet kiss, her thoughts fled until he broke away, smiled at her and closed the door.

After he'd proposed, he'd insisted they wait at least three months to get married. He wanted her to be sure about their commitment to each other. She'd *been* sure and had told him that over and over again. But Jed was a protective man as well as an old-fashioned one. Tonight they would make love for the first time, and she was so excited. Her anticipation made her longing even greater.

When Jed slid into the driver's seat, she eyed her new husband with all the pride and admiration she always felt for him. He was still wearing his tux and had never looked more handsome.

Sliding his hand under her hair, he brought her to him for another intoxicating kiss and then murmured, "There's a stop I want to make before we drive to Madison."

His kisses always left her in a daze. She blinked. "A stop?"

They were staying in Madison in a honeymoon suite for the next three nights. They really didn't have time for a long honeymoon, with the plans for the plastic surgery center taking up most of their time and Jed's involvement in getting a free clinic off the ground almost as exacting. They were both still working at the Beechwood Family Practice, having decided to stay there until the children's center was completed. They would work side by side to make it a success and the best facility of its kind in the United States.

For the past week, they'd readied an apartment that would suit them until they could find a house they liked. They'd toured a few, but none quite fit the bill. They were looking for something with a large bedroom on the first floor in case Al needed to move in with them. Brianne wondered if Jed's dad would ever give in and do that. He was so independent. When they'd broached the subject with Al, he'd grumbled that newlyweds didn't need an old codger around. But Brianne and Jed *did* need him around. She missed her parents and Al was quickly becoming a surrogate father. She loved him and had told him so before the wedding, to his blushing dismay.

Now Jed started the SUV and explained where he wanted to take her. "I found a house I want you to see. If you think it's right, we can put a deposit on it. I don't want someone to steal it out from under us."

Jed never took for granted that Brianne wanted the same things he did. When he asked her opinion, she truly felt like a partner.

To her surprise, Jed didn't turn into one of the newer developments but rather headed for an older section of Sawyer Springs. They stopped before a stately brick two-story.

"Does it have a bedroom on the first floor?" she asked.

"It has better than that."

Pulling into the driveway of the double car garage, he took a key from his pocket. "It's a good thing I knew the real estate agent from our high school days. I convinced her to let us look at it by ourselves. Come on."

When Jed led Brianne inside, she loved the older home immediately. It had been beautifully maintained. The hardwood floors were polished, the walls freshly painted, and the carved mahogany mantel was a highlight of the living room. Beautiful cherry-wood cabinets lined the kitchen. The appliances were new, down to the smooth-top stove. Colors from the spruce-green and off-white linoleum floor were picked up in the wallpaper above the sink and between the cupboards.

Jed crooked his finger at her, and she followed him

down a short hall. They passed a door that led to the garage. She was curious now.

He opened a second door and said, "This was added onto the back of the garage a few years ago. I think this could solve the problem of convincing Dad to move in."

When Jed opened the door, Brianne found herself walking into a sunny, spacious living room. There was a small kitchen area with an oven, space for a refrigerator, counter space for a microwave and a doorway that led into a bedroom.

"The bath even has a shower with one of those seats and hand-held units. And there's an intercom system."

Brianne crossed to Jed, slipped his arms under his coat and held on tight. "It's perfect."

"You haven't seen the rest of the house yet," he teased with a grin.

"We can look at that, too."

"There are four bedrooms...plenty of room for kids." Soon after Jed had proposed, they'd talked about having a family. Jed knew he could never replace Trisha, but he wanted more children to love. He wanted to be a dad again, and Brianne couldn't wait to be a mother.

"We'll fill this house with love and laughter," she promised.

With that intense expression on his face that she knew so well, with desire flaming brightly in the depths of his eyes, he nodded solemnly. The strength of his kiss repeated every promise they'd made earlier in the day. Brianne knew that Jed believed in the power of a solemn vow. She returned his vow with her own, knowing their future would be filled with love, passion, commitment and family.

When Jed raised his head, he winked at her. "This is only the beginning."

She lifted her face to his again, believing him, knowing their future had begun.

* * * * *

Watch for Karen Rose Smith's
Silhouette Special Edition
THEIR BABY BOND
in January 2004.

✂

Your opinion is important to us! Please take a few moments to share your thoughts with us about your experiences with Harlequin and Silhouette books. Your comments will be very useful in ensuring that we deliver books you love to read.
Please take a few minutes to complete the questionnaire, then send it to us at the address below.

Send your completed questionnaires to:
Harlequin/Silhouette Reader Survey, P.O. Box 9046, Buffalo, NY 14269-9046

---

1. As you may know, there are many different lines under the Harlequin and Silhouette brands. Each of the lines is listed below. Please check the box that most represents your reading habit for each line.

Line	Currently read this line	Do not read this line	Not sure if I read this line
Harlequin American Romance	❑	❑	❑
Harlequin Duets	❑	❑	❑
Harlequin Romance	❑	❑	❑
Harlequin Historicals	❑	❑	❑
Harlequin Superromance	❑	❑	❑
Harlequin Intrigue	❑	❑	❑
Harlequin Presents	❑	❑	❑
Harlequin Temptation	❑	❑	❑
Harlequin Blaze	❑	❑	❑
Silhouette Special Edition	❑	❑	❑
Silhouette Romance	❑	❑	❑
Silhouette Intimate Moments	❑	❑	❑
Silhouette Desire	❑	❑	❑

2. Which of the following best describes why you bought *this book?* One answer only, please.

the picture on the cover	❑	the title	❑
the author	❑	the line is one I read often	❑
part of a miniseries	❑	saw an ad in another book	❑
saw an ad in a magazine/newsletter	❑	a friend told me about it	❑
I borrowed/was given this book	❑	other: _____	❑

3. Where did you buy *this book?* One answer only, please.

at Barnes & Noble	❑	at a grocery store	❑
at Waldenbooks	❑	at a drugstore	❑
at Borders	❑	on eHarlequin.com Web site	❑
at another bookstore	❑	from another Web site	❑
at Wal-Mart	❑	Harlequin/Silhouette Reader	❑
at Target	❑	Service/through the mail	
at Kmart	❑	used books from anywhere	❑
at another department store or mass merchandiser	❑	I borrowed/was given this book	❑

4. On average, how many Harlequin and Silhouette books do you buy at one time?

I buy _____ books at one time ❑
I rarely buy a book ❑

MRQ403SR-1A

5. How many times per month do you shop for any *Harlequin and/or Silhouette* books?
One answer only, please.

1 or more times a week	❑	a few times per year ❑
1 to 3 times per month	❑	less often than once a year ❑
1 to 2 times every 3 months	❑	never ❑

6. When you think of your ideal heroine, which *one* statement describes her the best?
One answer only, please.

She's a woman who is strong-willed ❑	She's a desirable woman ❑
She's a woman who is needed by others ❑	She's a powerful woman ❑
She's a woman who is taken care of ❑	She's a passionate woman ❑
She's an adventurous woman ❑	She's a sensitive woman ❑

7. The following statements describe types or genres of books that you may be
interested in reading. Pick *up to 2 types* of books that you are most interested in.

I like to read about truly romantic relationships ❑
I like to read stories that are sexy romances ❑
I like to read romantic comedies ❑
I like to read a romantic mystery/suspense ❑
I like to read about romantic adventures ❑
I like to read romance stories that involve family ❑
I like to read about a romance in times or places that I have never seen ❑
Other: _____ ❑

*The following questions help us to group your answers with those readers who are
similar to you. Your answers will remain confidential.*

8. Please record your year of birth below.

19 ____

9. What is your marital status?

single ❑   married ❑   common-law ❑   widowed ❑
divorced/separated ❑

10. Do you have children 18 years of age or younger currently living at home?

yes ❑   no ❑

11. Which of the following best describes your employment status?

employed full-time or part-time ❑   homemaker ❑   student ❑
retired ❑   unemployed ❑

12. Do you have access to the Internet from either home or work?

yes ❑   no ❑

13. Have you ever visited eHarlequin.com?

yes ❑   no ❑

14. What state do you live in?

_____

15. Are you a member of Harlequin/Silhouette Reader Service?

yes ❑   Account # _____   no ❑   MRQ403SR-1B

If you enjoyed what you just read,
then we've got an offer you can't resist!

Take 2 bestselling love stories FREE!

Plus get a FREE surprise gift!

Clip this page and mail it to Silhouette Reader Service

IN U.S.A.
3010 Walden Ave.
P.O. Box 1867
Buffalo, N.Y. 14240-1867

IN CANADA
P.O. Box 609
Fort Erie, Ontario
L2A 5X3

YES! Please send me 2 free Silhouette Romance® novels and my free surprise gift. After receiving them, if I don't wish to receive anymore, I can return the shipping statement marked cancel. If I don't cancel, I will receive 6 brand-new novels every month, before they're available in stores! In the U.S.A., bill me at the bargain price of $21.34 per shipment plus 25¢ shipping and handling per book and applicable sales tax, if any*. In Canada, bill me at the bargain price of $24.68 plus 25¢ shipping and handling per book and applicable taxes**. That's the complete price and a savings of at least 10% off the cover prices—what a great deal! I understand that accepting the 2 free books and gift places me under no obligation ever to buy any books. I can always return a shipment and cancel at any time. Even if I never buy another book from Silhouette, the 2 free books and gift are mine to keep forever.

209 SDN DU9H
309 SDN DU9J

Name	(PLEASE PRINT)	
Address	Apt.#	
City	State/Prov.	Zip/Postal Code

* Terms and prices subject to change without notice. Sales tax applicable in N.Y.
** Canadian residents will be charged applicable provincial taxes and GST.
All orders subject to approval. Offer limited to one per household and not valid to current Silhouette Romance® subscribers.
® are registered trademarks of Harlequin Books S.A., used under license.

SROM03   ©1998 Harlequin Enterprises Limited

SILHOUETTE *Romance*®

COMING NEXT MONTH

#1694 FILL-IN FIANCÉE—DeAnna Talcott
Marrying the Boss's Daughter

Recruiting well-mannered beauty Sunny Robbins to pose as his bride-to-be was the perfect solution to Lord Breton Hamilton's biggest problem—his matchmaking parents! Sunny wasn't the titled English aristocrat they expected, but she was a more enticing alternative than *their* choices. And the way she sent his pulse racing… Was Brett's fill-in fiancée destined to become his lawfully—*lovingly*—wedded wife?

#1695 THE PRINCESS & THE MASKED MAN—
Valerie Parv
The Carramer Trust

Beautiful royals didn't propose marriages of convenience! Yet that's exactly what Princess Giselle de Marigny did when she discovered Bryce Laws's true identity. Since the widowed single father wanted a mother for his young daughter, he agreed to the plan. But Giselle's kisses stirred deeper feelings, and Bryce realized she might become keeper of his heart!

#1696 TO WED A SHEIK—Teresa Southwick
Desert Brides

Crown Prince Kamal Hassan promised never to succumb to the weakness of love, but Ali Matlock, his sexy new employee, was tempting him beyond all limits. The headstrong American had made it clear an office fling was out of the question. But for Kamal, so was giving up Ali. Would he trade his playboy lifestyle for a lifetime of happiness?

#1697 WEST TEXAS BRIDE—Madeline Baker

City girl Carly Kirkwood had about as much business on a Texas ranch as she did falling for rancher Zane Roan Eagle— none! Still, she couldn't deny her attraction to the handsome cowboy or the sparks that flew between them. Would she be able to leave the big city behind for Zane? And could she forgive him when the secrets of his past were revealed?

SRCNM1003